THE MARLEY DIARIES

VASALONA COOPER

Copyright © 2021 by Vasalona Cooper

All rights reserved.

No part of this book may be reproduced in any form or by any electronic or mechanical means, including information storage and retrieval systems, without written permission from the author, except for the use of brief quotations in a book review.

Published: Vasalona Cooper 2021

Cover Design: Murphy Rae www.murphyrae.net

❦ Created with Vellum

To my true believers.
Thanks for never giving up on me. I recognize you and love you for all your support.

THE MARLEY DIARIES

The trees are about to show you just how beautiful letting go can be.

HERMAN HESSE

WELLNESS

I

Sunday, September 9

Wellness Resorts seem to be all the rage right now or maybe they always have been, and I'm just slowing down long enough to catch on. I read somewhere that Oprah frequented this very resort, and I was hoping I'd catch her walking by in an expensive lavender jogger; her curls brushed back in a matching headband. She'd recognize me as the editor-in-chief of Mod magazine, and we'd laugh and joke over herbal tea and avocado toast with fresh fruit from the resort's garden. I'd sneak in an interview for the mag's hot topics section. Oprah would playfully scold me for working when I was really supposed to be letting myself go, taking a breather, and relishing in all the luxuries the high-end spa had to offer.

I'd tell Oprah that I'm here because I'm emotionally, physically, and mentally burned out. Sad that it took a break-up to realize it. Maybe she'd have some ratchet break-up stories to spill about Stedman; the thought alone made me laugh. I couldn't see a man like him doing anything wrong, but who am I to judge? I didn't think my ex would break up with me.

I'd dated Trey Ellis an entire year, and in those 12 months, our relationship had been blissful, fun, and so gratifying. We'd never gotten into an argument, which is why I didn't understand his reasoning for leaving me.

I had devised different scenarios over and over in my head to pinpoint where things could have gone wrong; where I went wrong! His break-up speech sounded like a rendition of *"Where I Wanna Be"* by Donell Jones. I was flabbergasted. After Trey broke the news, I sat there wondering if he was playing a joke on me, but when that single pathetic tear fell from his eyes, I knew he was serious. I couldn't believe it. I was stunned. But the last thing I wanted to do was play the victim. Hell, apparently, I'd already been playing the fool, and it took everything in me to pretend the feeling was mutual, that I too needed some space.

After that, I buried myself in work to help me get over the torment. I attended every invite I was handed, mostly launch parties and awards shows. I even went back to online dating, which is one of the most energy-sucking ways to meet a guy ever. None of them made it past the "exchanging phone numbers to meet in person" stage. It was a bunch of boring conversations. Some of the conversations seemed to be pre-written and copied and pasted from one girl to the next and then straight to me.

And let's not forget about the men who couldn't spell, the men who never wrote back, or the men who only wanted you to follow them on their social media. It seemed like dating had turned into a got damn circus and I wasn't impressed.

Time tried its hardest to heal the wound Trey had left me with when he walked out of my life. No matter how much I seemed to get over him, I still couldn't stop thinking about him. He was grounded in the back of my mind like a bittersweet memory. This wellness retreat would be everything I needed and then some. I made a promise to enjoy this new journey with my inner self. And while I trekked on this new adventure, I would cleanse myself of the bitterness, gain new insight on my purpose in life, and simply get back to being me. Fun, healthy, ambitious, Marley.

TEQUILA

2

Monday, September 24

I walked through the doors of Moon Publishing, feeling a sense of renewed and refreshed energy. I knew it had a lot to do with my *"vacation"*, but I also loved my job. Every time I stepped out of those elevator doors and onto the glossy, pristine marble floors, I'd get an overwhelming sense of excitement. The receptionist Brit, whose station sat in the middle of an opulent lobby, always made sure to adorn the counters with fresh flowers so elaborate they fragranced the entire room.

The heavy glass doors behind her desk lead to the offices of editors, journalists, executives, and me, the editor-in-chief of Mod Magazine. Mod was printed monthly right here in Savannah, GA., and covered beauty, fashion, entertainment, and culture. We were a big deal, sitting on shelves next to Vogue and Marie Claire. We were often compared to magazines like Essence and Cosmopolitan.

No sooner than I collected my mail from Brit and walked through the door was I bombarded by my best friend, Lo.

"Welcome back," she greeted with a pinch of sarcasm in her voice.

"I missed you."

Lo rolled her eyes. "Did that self-care thingy serve its purpose?"

"*Wellness* Retreat," I corrected her. "And yes!"

"Good. I'm glad you got some peace. I think ignoring my calls was a bit dramatic, but whatever," she shrugged.

"They had a no-phone policy. I wasn't ignoring you. Besides, I called you as soon as I got back from Arizona. You sent my call to voicemail."

"Oh yeah," she pondered. "You called around the time I was getting my ear chewed off by Mitch the Bitch. He's on my department's ass for story slacking."

"You're the best gossip columnist here. How are you slacking?"

"He thinks our stories are passé, and in a way, he's right. None of our shit is really original. It's piggy backing off the next blog or magazine's news stories. Mod is supposed to have the hottest entertainment out there. And we did once upon a time."

"If you feel like the journalist need to step their game

up, then we'll have another meeting about it. I want to be there."

"Great. I'll let Mitch know."

I shuffled through my mail as we rounded the corner. Lo's short legs managed to keep up with my long strides as we headed towards my office door.

"Um. Sooo..." she dragged out, stalling to finish her sentence.

"So?" I asked.

"I have something to tell you, but promise me you won't freak out when I say it."

"Too late. I'm already freaking out," I scoffed. "What is it? Because if it has to do with work, wait until I've had my coffee, please."

"Okay, well, I talked to Allan last night."

"I thought you two broke up?"

"We did, but..." Lo shook her head violently. "That's not the point. Allan told me something. Something about Trey."

Just the mention of his name made me stop in my tracks. I looked at Lo, my face drawing with curiosity. It wasn't until then that I realized she had changed her hair. The wavy haircut I'd last seen her sporting was replaced with braids in different hues of browns and blondes that hung past her waist.

She looked panicky, her eyes bouncing and looking everywhere but at me.

"Lo," I called gently. "What did he say?"

"Trey is getting married." She said it carefully as if she hated to be the bearer of bad news.

"Oh," I said softly. My chest felt like it was in a vice grip.

Lo studied me for a moment. My face contorted into an expression that showed I could care less but deep down, I was aching and hella confused.

"Are you okay?"

Uh, no!

Trey had just broken up with me less than three months ago, and he'd already found someone he wanted to marry? I wasn't even dating! During our hiatus, I'd assumed Trey would have come to his senses and then come running back to me. But he'd run into the arms of someone else.

I stormed away, making a beeline to my office, whizzing by offices and cubicles.

"Marley?"

Lo closed the door behind us once we were in my office and put her hands on her 35-inch hips. "Talk to me."

"I'm good."

"Are you sure? Because you look like you stumped your toe on a coffee table."

I feigned a bright smile and took a deep breath. "I'm fine. That's what my vacation was all about. Letting go and finding my inner peace. I'm. Good." I assured myself. I took a seat at my desk. The comfort of my task chair felt good, and I was eager to get back to work.

"And I'm happy for Trey," I managed. "I think it's perfect. If that's what he wants." I woke up my Mac and started reading through emails. When Lo didn't respond, I looked up to see her staring at me like I had three heads.

"What?" I quipped.

She sucked her teeth, and just as she was about to open her mouth to speak, a soft tap at the door stopped her. It was my assistant Andy. "Welcome back, Ms. Jacobs. Here's your coffee."

She smiled hello at Lo and then set the steaming mug of caffeine on the edge of my desk.

"Thank you, Andy."

"No problem. I just wanted to remind you that the launch party for Cherokee Rose Wholistics is tomorrow evening at six. You also have a meeting today with Owen Daniels at 11:30, and Taraji wants to reschedule the interview for next week Wednesday at two o'clock."

"Ok, that's perfect."

I blew in the coffee mug in an attempt to cool it off before taking a sip. Like always Andy made it just right, but the caffeine did nothing to settle the strain I was feeling. I needed something stronger, like a shot of tequila.

"Is there anything else you need?" Andy asked politely.

"Yes. Arrange a meeting with all the gossip columnists for next week Thursday."

She nodded. "I'll get right on it."

"Thanks, Andy!"

"No problem," she beamed before disappearing from my office. Lo waited until the door clicked before she rolled her neck around and glared at me.

"Okay, you can play pretend all day if that's what you

want, but you have to be simmering inside, Marley. I know you!"

"Maybe I am. And maybe *now* is not the best time to discuss this!"

"Okay," Lo grunted and crossed her arms in front of her. "You're right. I've got some calls I need to make. But you and I are going to talk about this later." She narrowed her eyes at me and pointed her black acrylic nails in my direction. It was like a scene out of the *Color Purple* when Ciely pointed her two crooked fingers at Mister.

I nodded.

Lo left.

My shoulders slumped as I threw my head back against my chair, willing myself not to break down... again. Lo's words echoed in my brain.

Trey is getting married.

Trey is getting married?!

I'd just gotten over our break-up. Now, this?! More Trey drama! It was almost as if he were purposely trying to torment me. Married to who? Who was this woman that won his heart so suddenly? I scooted closer to my desk and logged into my Facebook account. I was frustrated when I couldn't find Trey's profile but then remembered I had him blocked.

I unblocked his page, and I didn't have to look far before I had my answer confirmed. Trey's profile picture was a beautiful photograph of him and his fiancée grinning from ear to ear. He stood behind her, his muscular arms wrapped around her slender waist and his lips kissing her rouged cheek. Her hazel eyes sparkled behind square-framed glasses. I hated to admit how good they looked together.

I felt tiny needles of jealousy stabbing my heart. I grew angry, and before I knew it, I was dialing Trey's number. I had planned to scream and shout how insensitive he was, but the sound of his baritone when he said *hello* changed all of that. Just that quick, I had no words to say. I started to hang up, but he called my name so sweetly, it nearly brought a tear to my eye.

"Hi," I said, trying to keep myself in control.

"I've missed you," he told me, catching me off guard. "I'm so glad you called. I've wanted to call you, but I-I don't know. How are you?" he asked, suddenly sounding nervous.

"I'm good. I'm really good!" I exaggerated.

"Great. That's great!"

"I know, right. Things are great."

"That's awesome."

"I know." I rubbed my forehead out of pure embarrassment. What the hell was I talking about?

An awkward silence hung over us. So many questions were going through my head, and I was too afraid to voice them out loud in fear of getting answers that would cut me to the core. Like, where and when did he meet that librarian-looking girl?

Trey cleared his throat and said, "I guess I should tell you that I'm uh-I'm... I'm getting married."

I pretended to be surprised. "Oh wow! That's amazing!"

"Yeah! Wait... really?" He asked. Disbelief was tinged in his voice.

"Yeah, I'm happy for you!"

Trey scoffed, probably not buying one bit of the overjoyed performance I was putting on. "OK," he said weakly.

"What's wrong, Trey? Aren't you happy? Isn't this what you want?" I couldn't get the bitter sarcasm out of my voice if I tried.

"I guess I just didn't expect you to be so... happy."

"Why wouldn't I be?"

"Because we, well, I mean..." He didn't finish. Instead, he cleared his throat. "I'm glad we could end things on a good note."

"I mean, not good enough that I want to be a guest at your wedding," I teased. Trey laughed. I pictured him with his head thrown back, his Adam's apple bobbing with each chuckle.

"No, I wouldn't go so far as to do that," he said with a smile in his voice.

"It would be a flat-out no, just so you know. But when is the big day?" I asked.

"The big day is in February. I don't know if I'm ready, to be honest."

My heart dropped to the floor. There was no masking my surprise. It felt like someone had punched me in the chest.

"February, Trey? As in five months from now, February? That's really fast. We just broke up," I argued. What I really wanted to say was that we dated for a year and we never so much as mentioned getting engaged to one another.

"A lot can happen in three months, Mar."

"I see!"

"Wait a minute; I thought you said you were happy for me?"

"Yeah, I was, until I found out you're getting married in five months!"

"Five months, five years. Does it really matter?"

"I guess not. Look, congratulations, Trey, but I need to go. There's so much work I have to-"

"Marley, wait. Can we talk? I have to see you."

I paused.

"I meant it when I said I missed you. You've been on my mind like crazy. I have to see you, before... please," he pleaded.

My mind felt like it was in a whirlpool. I was livid, sad, and confused all at the same time. What the hell was going on? There was nothing else for us to talk about. There was nothing else left for us to do.

He's engaged to another woman.

It's over between us. He'd made that clear three months ago. I wanted to tell Trey to go to hell, but I swallowed my strength when he asked, "Can you meet me at the Pink House tonight?"

"Trey," I called out to him.

"Please. Just dinner. I promise."

"Alright," I quivered. My voice was barely above a whisper, but he'd heard it.

"Great, thank you! Seven o'clock, okay? And don't be

late," he said before I could change my mind. The call ended, and I cradled my cell phone to my chest, wondering why I'd agreed to meet the man who broke my heart. I shouldn't be doing this, I thought to myself, but for some reason, an enticing smile graced my lips.

MINE

3

Monday, September 24

I swear my little sister's timing couldn't have been more off than it was now. She called me just as I was heading to my beautician to get my hair done.

"Jinni, is everything good?" I asked. She sounded like she'd been crying.

"Are you home?"

"Downtown" I answered.

"I'm on my way to your house," she sniffled. It was just like her to not care what I was doing. When Jinni needed me, she needed me, and everything else could wait.

I rushed home, staring at my Cartier watch every five seconds and praying my sister's visit wouldn't be a long one. I only had two hours before it was time to meet Trey and I didn't even know what I was going to wear. Getting my hair straightened was out of the question now.

Jinni's Range Rover was parked in my driveway when I made it home. She was standing on my front porch smoking a cigarette and tapping her foot impatiently. There was an overnight bag by her feet. I shook my head and got out of my car, knowing good and damn well what this was all about.

"Took you long enough!" she hissed, then dropped the half-smoked cigarette in front of her and stomped it with the ball of her Gucci sneakers.

She nearly knocked me over when she followed me into the house. Jinni went straight to the kitchen as I dragged myself like a bratty child across the floor into the living room. I plopped myself and my bags on my blush-colored loveseat and closed my eyes, waiting for what I knew would be the downpour of Donovan's latest antics.

"You don't have anything stronger than this?" Jinni marched into the living room with two rose-colored flutes and a bottle of Veuve Cliquot I didn't get the chance to open yet.

Her face looked disgusted as she took a seat on the sofa across from me.

"No. I don't. And I thought you quit smoking?"

"Some habits are hard to break." I watched her shaky hands pour our drinks, her large emerald cut diamond ring flashing so bright I wondered if she'd just had it cleaned.

"Okay... so what happened?" I asked, trying to move things along. Jinni cut her eyes at me while she handed me a glass. She took a hard swallow of her champagne before uttering the words, "Donovan is cheating on me again."

"Damn," I sighed. I tried hard to sound sincere, but I wasn't the least bit surprised. Donovan Sheppard, former NBA player, was always cheating on Jinni, and Jinni was always taking him back. Donovan's apologies always came with the latest Hermes bag or a luxury car.

"I'm leaving him," Jinni said in a low, determined voice. "I'm filing for divorce tomorrow."

I nearly choked. I'd heard a lot of things from my sister about her and Donovan's toxic relationship, but never once had Jinni mentioned *that* word.

"Divorce? Wow, Jinni, are you sure that's what you want to do?"

"I'm sure."

"What changed?" I probed.

"His latest hoe is pregnant. There's no coming back from that," her lips started to tremble and tears began to pour from her eyes. I was at my sister's side within seconds, holding her and hugging her as she wept and wailed.

"What am I going to tell the kids?" Jinni bleated. My heart ached as I thought of my nieces and nephew.

"Tell them the truth! There isn't going to be an easy way. And you're going to have to do it before someone finds out and leaks this to the press."

She sniffles. "You're right. I'm just shocked that

tramp hasn't told anyone yet. Most women can't wait to tell the world that they slept with my husband. She must really love him."

"Or maybe Donovan is paying her to be quiet. She could have signed a non-disclosure. Do you think he's serious about her?" I asked. My journalist psyche kicked in and I started itching to get a pen and pad.

"The bitch's coochie must be made of kryptonite. Donny's not even focused on me and the kids. It's been that way for months. We don't even talk anymore. I barely see him."

"Who is she? Is she famous?"

"I'm not sure," Jinni fumed.

"Then how do you know she's pregnant?"

Jinni gave me an odd look; her eyes were red and puffy. "Am I talking to sister Marley or journalist Marley?" she snapped and then her voice grew loud and aggressive. "I saw the text messages! They've been talking since March. I don't know her name. Donny's got her listed as bae in his phone!" She started wailing again. The hurt expression on her face was enough to make me shed a tear. "Jinni, I'm so sorry," I told her. I tried to find the optimism in this, but I was at a loss for words.

I sat with Jinni all night while she talked, cried, and drank herself into a drunken stupor. Once her eyes shut and she drifted off into a deep sleep, I tucked her in on the sofa, placing a throw cover over her body. I brought the empty champagne bottle and flutes into the kitchen. As I washed the glasses, I pondered on the misery my sister was going through, and, in a flash, Trey came to mind.

Trey!

I'd forgotten all about him and our date. I raced to my purse, searching for my cell phone. There were three missed calls and five text messages from him.

Did you change your mind?

I'll wait ten more minutes.

Are you okay?

I'm still here. Just tell me you're okay.

Alright, I understand.

My fingers couldn't dial his number fast enough. When I finally managed to get it right, my call went straight to voicemail. I groaned and tossed the phone on the armchair.

Damn it!

It was nine o'clock. I covered my face with my hands then ran my fingers through my natural coils. Trey probably thought I'd purposely stood him up, the whole while I was catering to my spoiled little sister.

I looked over at Jinni, sleeping peacefully on the couch, and told myself it was for the best. Trey was going to be a married man, and after what Jinni just told me, I didn't want to play the same role as the home wrecker who'd just helped ruin her marriage with Donovan.

I undressed to take a shower, turning the dials until I got the right water temperature. I couldn't even get a toe in before a hard knock on my front door sounded. It was so loud I nearly jumped out of my skin. I turned the water off before I reached for my black satin robe hanging behind the bathroom door. I slipped my arms through the sleeves and rushed into the living room, tying the belt of the robe around my waist. Jinni was still in a deep sleep, snoring like a bear cub. The knocking started up again.

"Marley, open up, it's me!" Trey's voice boomed from the other side of the door.

"Trey?" He took my breath away when I opened the door and saw him standing there, almost as tall as the door frame. He looked dumbstruck; his eyes scanned over me as if seeing me for the first time. When our eyes locked, my heart skipped a beat. I wanted to reach out and hug him, caress him, claw his eyes out.

"What are you doing here?" I could barely recognize my own voice; muddled and frigid.

"I needed to see you."

"Why?"

His face was so handsome, carved to perfection and it irked me that I'd no longer be the one to see it every day, kiss it every day, or sit on it... every day. I loved him, still love him, and the fact that he stopped loving me was like a dagger to my soul.

Before I knew it, I'd slapped Trey so hard my hand felt like it was on fire, but that didn't stop me from slapping him again. And again. I erupted, beating Trey in the chest with my balled-up fists, screaming at him, shouting, forgetting to keep the noise level down for my sleeping sister.

"You embarrassed me!" I thundered. "Why love me and then leave me like that? Was any of it real?"

Trey seemed undaunted by my blows and caught

each of my wrists in his burly hands. He stepped into the foyer, leaving me no choice but to step backward. He closed the door with his foot. With his grip still on my wrist, he managed to fold them behind my back and pull me close to him at the same time. That handsome face lowered towards me and Trey shushed my mouth with his. I felt myself calm in an instant, kissing him back with soft, slow pecks.

"I'm sorry, Marley. I'm so, so sorry," Trey whispered with his lips pressed close to mine. His breath smelled like sweet cranberries and vodka. His tongue lightly brushed my lower lip, testing me to see if I wanted it. My body pulsed. It cried out for him. I could feel myself giving in slowly but surely. I definitely wanted it. I needed it. I needed him.

"Trust me; it was real. It was all real," he breathed. His lips were on my neck now. Trey hadn't touched the most delicate part of me yet and already I was wetter than a cucumber in a women's prison.

I let all my inhibitions loose when he lifted me in his arms and wrapped my legs around his waist. I clung to him like a spider monkey, kissing him with everything I had in me. The left side of my robe fell from my shoulder and Trey placed soft pecks from his full mouth on my collarbone, sending tremors down my spine. I ran my fingers through his hair as he carried me down the hall to my bedroom.

The look in his eyes as he laid me across my king-size bed made my nipples harden. It was an intense look of passion. Like I amazed him.

He untied my robe, exposing the rest of my nakedness. He pushed my knees back and buried his head between my legs. Sweet kisses were planted on my inner thigh until his mouth found my honey pot. I massaged the back of his head, aching to have him further and deeper inside of me. His tongue played with my clit and within two minutes, I came harder than I ever came before, but he didn't stop. He kept licking and stroking me with his tongue until I thought I'd lose my mind.

"Ohmigod, Trey!"

"That's right, baby, cum for me. All over this tongue," he groaned.

My legs shook. I couldn't stop the uncontrollable shaking of my body as I lost all self-control and rained down on his face. "Trey!" I pushed his forehead back gently, not able to take any more of the satisfaction he was giving.

"You want me to stop," he smirked.

"I need to feel you inside me."

Trey's thick manhood throbbed as he stood up. My chest caved in hard as I anxiously waited for what I'd been missing. When he finally pushed inside my moist pussy, I felt high off desire. He pounded into me with strong, deep strokes. "Don't stop, Trey. I missed you."

"I missed you too, Marley. I love you," he moaned breathlessly.

The words took me by surprise. I searched Trey's eyes for deceit, but he stared back at me with genuineness. It was music to my ears.

At that moment, it was confirmed that I was his and

he was mine, and there would be no more *her*. I rolled over on top of him and licked my way down his chiseled stomach, seizing a mouthful of his stiff dick inside my mouth.

Yes.

Trey was all mine.

CLOSURE

4

Tuesday, September 25

In the morning, after I woke up to an empty bed and the smell of bacon, I stretched and smiled. How fast things had gone back to the way they were when Trey and I were together. Passionate sex all night and then waking up to the smell of Trey cooking breakfast in the morning.

I grabbed the robe Trey had ripped off me last night and put it back on as I walked down the hall, my feet tiptoeing on the cold hardwood floors.

Jinni whipping a bowl of eggs was the last thing I expected to see as I rounded the corner and entered the kitchen. She turned, startled by my presence. "Oh, hey." She went back to cooking. "How'd you sleep?" she asked teasingly.

"Good," I answered in disappointment. I hugged

myself, feeling exposed and embarrassed. Jinni looked over her shoulder and chuckled when she saw my eyes darting here, there, and everywhere.

"You looking for Trey? He snuck out fifteen minutes ago."

"Oh," I sighed.

"When did you two get back together? I thought y'all broke up." she pondered; her brow furrowed.

"Um, yeah... we did. I guess, we just..." but I didn't know how to explain it.

"Breakup sex?" she asked. I looked at her, appalled.

Was it?

Jinni chuckled again and rolled her eyes before turning back to the breakfast she was preparing. "Breakup sex is a good thing. Well, sometimes. But trust me, it does help you with closure."

"Closure?" I repeated. Was that what last night was about? Trey needing closure before he ran off into the sunset with his bride? Some kind of finale fuck for him to get peace of mind before moving on with little miss spectacles?

I felt like the wind had been knocked out of me, so I sat down at the kitchen table. My mind kept going over everything he did to me last night, everything he said. He told me he loved me. Was that a lie? How could he make love to me like that and not love me?

Jinni started rambling, going on about the sex sessions she'd have with Donovan after the two of them would break up or have a huge fight. I listened with profound interest and by the time she'd finished listing the pros and cons of it, she'd finished making grits, frying bacon, and scrambling eggs.

"I guess once you think of it, it's really not the best thing to do," Jinni shrugged. "The weaker one in the relationship ends up getting hurt because the one with the power leaves feeling confident and in control, knowing he or she doesn't want to get back together. They just wanted the sex."

She stopped what she was doing and smiled to herself. "I should have finished school. I would have been one hell of a therapist," she laughed and joined me at the kitchen table. Steam rising off the food she'd placed in front of us.

"What happened between the two of you, anyway? You never told me."

"Because I was too angry to talk about it. It was..." I sighed. "A lot of things were left unsaid. No explanation, really."

"Is that why he came over last night? To explain himself," she popped a piece of bacon in her mouth and smirked.

I rolled my eyes.

"Damn, you still got it bad, huh?" Jinni frowned.

"It's fine," I stopped her. "I'm fine. I don't know what last night meant. I mean, I should have known. He's got a whole fiancée-"

"Wait. What?" Jinni dropped her fork on her plate so hard I thought it would break my glassware. "Trey is engaged?"

I nodded. My sister gave me an incredulous look and

then coughed out a short laugh. She scooted away from the table, her chair screeching loudly across the floor. "Wow." She stood up, her hands on her hips, looking at me like I was a disobedient child. "What is with you women fucking men that don't belong to you?"

I looked at Jinni, baffled. "Excuse me?"

"Women like you are the reason I'm so bitter right now. You can have any man you want, Marley. Look at you! You're beautiful, successful. A fucking editor for a global magazine! And you choose to pursue someone that has a fiancée."

"Okay! Trey is not just someone. He was mine first!" I didn't mean to shout... or sound like a toddler. "And my situation is nothing like yours. He doesn't have a wife and kids at home."

"Maybe not! But he's still committed to someone he wants to make his wife!"

My body tensed up. Jinni might as well have slapped me across the face. She dropped her head in her hand, looking disappointed and betrayed.

"Things between Trey and I are complicated right now, but he is not married."

"Okay, engaged!" Jinni countered and rolled her eyes as if it didn't make a difference to her one way or another.

I wanted to strangle her. "That's not the same!"

"Damn near."

"Not! The same!" I yelled. I was mortified. My sister was acting like I was the one sleeping with Donovan. I don't know if I was hurt by Jinni or hurt by the truth. No, Trey wasn't married, but he had one foot in. He earmarked a relationship with a woman he saw a future with. He hadn't done that with me and we'd been together a lot longer.

I felt silly for forgiving him so easily, for letting my heart and my legs open back up to him. I wished the feeling of me craving him would go away, but it lingered in the core of me.

I didn't realize I was crying until Jinni hugged me. She cried too, and I couldn't decide if it was for my pain or hers. The two of us, broken-hearted sisters, crying over men who'd brought us up and broken us down.

Jinni spent the rest of the day in my guest bedroom and I'd escaped to my room to think. I was feeling worse than when Lo told me Trey was getting married. I felt violated. Used. I kept picturing Trey running back to her right after he'd left my bed, and that put a dent in my heart so bad I nearly screamed.

I took a shower, letting the hot water slip down my body in hopes it would rinse away all the regret I'd been feeling. The water soothed me, but it didn't erase my bitter thoughts.

I washed the sheets on my bed, and I thought about the million and one things I needed to do. There was no time to sulk. I needed to call Andy and have her set up an impromptu meeting with my fashion team, but I noticed my cell phone wasn't in my room. It took me almost five minutes to remember I threw it somewhere in the living room last night. When I found it lying on the loveseat, I snatched it up to read the time, but Trey's name was illuminated across the screen. He'd left a text over an hour ago. You were snoring like a bear so I didn't want to wake you. I'm out of town on business until next week. Let's do dinner when I get back and don't be a no-show this time. *wink face*. I'll explain everything in person. Promise.

You're damn right you will.

JITTERS

5

Friday, September 28

The next couple of days consisted of analyzing and making decisions for Mod for hours on end, but it didn't feel like work because I was doing what I loved; managing a magazine, and dealing with endless dilemmas, which oddly felt stimulating.

The meeting with Lo, Mitch, and the gossip columnist went better than expected. Everyone seemed on board knowing Mod needed stories that didn't seem recycled from our lead competitors. Lo left feeling relieved and so upbeat she wanted to treat me and our friends, Gia and Harper, to lunch.

We met at our usual spot downtown on Broughton St. and by 1:30, the four of us were gathered at our favorite table at Chive Sea Bar, listening to Gia explain the horrid tales of her birthday planning.

"It's a family-owned business, which I love, but don't tell me you're delivering food for over 200 guests in a damn Chevy Malibu! Gia piped. We snorted with laughter; Harper almost fell out of her chair. Gia's face didn't even crack. She was serious and didn't find not one bit of what she just said amusing. "It's not funny. It's tacky! And on top of not having a food delivery truck, they aren't providing half the things that were agreed upon in the contract."

"Where the hell did you find these people?" Lo snickered.

"They're Lyle's cousins! I swear I have the cheapest husband on the planet." Gia popped another piece of bread in her mouth and waited until she was done chewing to finish her rant. "I didn't think finding someone to cook and deliver some food would be so hard, but he can't even do that."

Gia Baskin married her high school sweetheart, Lyle, who is a successful software developer. They live an honest-to-goodness, picture-perfect life. Like... honestly. Gia is a talented singer that recently signed with a famous record label. Her hit single, "I Wonder" sounded like a mixture of Erykah Badu and Ari Lennox. The funky jazz song even earned Gia a Grammy nomination.

"Give Lyle a break. He was only trying to help," Harper stated.

"But that is cutting it close," I marveled. "Who are you going to find on such short notice?"

"I don't know. A few people are supposed to be emailing me back before the end of the day," Gia sighed.

Despite the amount of stress Gia appeared to be under, her pecan brown skin was glowing against her cream cable-knit sweater. She reached in the breadbasket for her fourth complimentary bread roll.

"Well, I can't wait to introduce you guys to my boy toy. I might bring him with me to the party," Harper squirmed.

"Yasssss," Lo buzzed. "I've been waiting to meet this walking sex beast."

"I don't understand you, Harper. How do you go from a man winning Grammy awards to a man with no job?" Gia asked in actual concern.

"Sis, trust me, my reasons have nothing to do with finances," Harper grinned like a Cheshire cat.

As always, Harper Evergreen is unfazed by the criticism. She ended her marriage to a music producer six months ago and has been living her best life dating some super sexy model paparazzi couldn't stop taking pictures of.

"What's wrong with being with a man for fun and fun only? Everything doesn't have to be about finding a man to be committed to," Lo pitched in. She tossed her skinny braids over her shoulder before finishing off her tequila sunrise, our drink of choice during our social gatherings.

"This coming from a woman who hasn't been committed to a man in over a year."

Lo pretended to be offended. "Excuse me for basking in my singleness and loving it. The more time I spend alone, the more I realize I enjoy my peace. I'm good over here. Trust."

"We're women and we have feelings," Gia countered. "You mean to tell me you don't ever get caught up, trying to make a fling or a booty call something more than what it is?"

Lo and Harper looked at each other with blank expressions and then back at Gia.

"No," they chirped with a shrug of their shoulders. I giggled.

"But he doesn't have a job?" Gia stated with a frown and a confused look on her face.

"He doesn't need one!" Lo and Harper both snapped in unison. They broke out into a fit of laughter and gave each other a high-five from across the table. Gia rolled her eyes, clearly looking annoyed with the two of them.

"I don't need Tony to buy me anything. I just need the dick!" Harper crooned.

"You guys are sick," I teased. Our food finally arrived and the waitress set the delicious meals in front of us. I made sure to order another round of tequila sunrises before she walked away.

I was smiling and digging into my crab cake when Harper said, "Marley don't think for one minute I haven't noticed you sitting over there with that coy look on your face."

"I know, right. I noticed it too. New smile, who dis?" Gia teased.

"Who sent you those flowers yesterday?" asked Lo, shoving a forkful of mashed sweet potatoes in her mouth.

There was a vexing grin spread across her mouth as she chewed, and I wanted to smack it right off her face. She ignored my death stare and turned to Harper and Gia. "This big ass planter with a rose bush in it gets delivered to the office yesterday, right? I'm thinking it's to decorate the staff room, but no... it's for Marley. This big ass bush! And she won't tell me anything."

"Well, damn, that's what I'm talking about!" Harper exclaimed. "I can't even get a bouquet, let alone a damn bush."

"That's because your man doesn't have a job," Gia cracked.

We laughed, even Harper, who pushed Gia's shoulder playfully. "Shut up."

Lo eyes me over her food, waiting for my answer. "Is that what you've been up to lately. Canoodling with a rebound?"

"Is he cute?"

"Hopefully, he can get your mind off Trey," Harper added.

My cheeks flushed with embarrassment.

Lo, who knows me better than anyone else, peeped my body language. Her eyes widened with surprise and then she shook her head in disappointment. "Did those flowers come from Trey?" she asked.

The answer is written all over my blushing face.

Yes, the flowers had come from Trey. We'd been texting each other every day since our last night together. Joking about everything, laughing about everything, and talking about everything... well, everything except what needed to be talked about. I was purposely avoiding it like the plague or maybe he was too. Fear of knowing the truth stopped me from asking the obvious.

"Wait, you're serious?" That came from Harper, who almost choked on her BLT.

"How did that happen?" This from Gia, who has that frown and screwy confused look on her face again. And then there is Lo again, whacking that final nail in the coffin. "I thought Trey was getting married in like, five weeks."

"Five months," I corrected her.

"So, the wedding is off now?" she asked.

"Yeah," I said, but my voice cracked in uncertainty.

Lo shifted next to me, shuffling the food around on her plate before shaking her head again in a way that showed she pitied me.

I tell my girlfriends about the night Trey and I reunited. Gia gawked at me, hanging on to my every word as I finished off on how Trey and I ended the night.

"Oh, Marley," she sighed.

"Yeah. And it's been like old times ever since. I'm assuming he broke up with her."

"Okay, but what was his explanation for breaking up with you?" Lo quipped. "He literally broke up with you on some humbug shit and then proposed to another woman. A white woman at that. I know that's gotta be a shot to your ego."

I dropped my head, my fork frisking my rice pilaf. Seeing Trey's fiancée with the same fair-colored complexion as his hit an insecurity button inside of me.

We were total opposites. Her skin was milky white and mine was buttery brown. Her hair was golden and silky and mine was coarse and stretching out to the sun.

"It did catch me off guard, but Trey isn't like that. It was never a fetish type thing. We genuinely liked each other," I told them.

Our cocktails arrived and we all took long gulps, everyone except for Gia, who claimed to be on diet until her birthday. She was eating some kind of seaweed salad with fruit and drinking water.

"What do you think it is?"

I shrugged. "I don't know. And at this point, honestly guys, I don't care. Things are fine right now. I'm just going with the flow, and the flow is good. We FaceTime and text so much, it's like that girl is doesn't even exist," I added.

"That's usually how it is," Harper feigned a smile. "When Jason was cheating on me, I thought to myself, how did he find the time? But these men will find a way."

"I agree," Lo added. "Men have a way of making us weak.

Harper rolled her eyes. "Do men have us weak? Or do we just get stupid over the wrong men?

"Maybe it's both. Some of us get so head over heels that we start letting men control our minds and our bodies," Lo preached.

I waved my hand in the air. "Guys, I'm right here! And I'm not so far gone that I'm letting Trey control anything."

"We never think we are until it's too late," Harper giggled drunkenly.

"When the two of you meet again, let him explain himself but don't sleep with him. A piece of me thinks Trey is going through the jitters."

"Jitters? Like, wedding jitters?"

"Lo, please. It's not wedding jitters," Harper commented. "That man is not confused. I refuse to believe he came to his senses once they started talking about seating arrangements and color swatches."

Lo raised her glass in agreement then took a sip.

"And who's to say this girl is the rebound chick? How do we know Trey wasn't dating this broad while he was talking to Marley," Harper finished.

My bottom lip dropped. Even Lo and Gia looked offended. Harper winced, cringing like she'd take her harsh words back in a second if she could. "Damn it, Marley. I'm sorry. You know these drinks make me-"

"You're good," I told her. But it became embedded in my mind. Trey dating before we broke up?

Lo and Gia looked at me as if I'd been wounded and in a way, I had. Truth hurts. I mean, if it was the truth.

BLACK

6

Tuesday, October 2

Jinni was sleeping on my living room sofa when I got home from work. The TV was on, the volume was high, but no one was watching it. Her twelve-year-old son, DJ, was sitting at her feet, playing a handheld video game. The twins, Elle, and Everley were lying on my white Persian rug coloring in a coloring book with markers. My body tensed as my eyes roamed the rug for colorful marks. When I saw none, I cleared my throat. "Girls. Can you two finish coloring at the table? Please." I gave a patient smile. My nieces, both six years old, let out a deep irritated sigh before moving their artwork and supplies to the kitchen table.

I looked around at the toys, children's books, and my throw pillows from my couch scattered all over the living room. Candy wrappers, cups, and Happy Meal Boxes were spread out on top of the coffee table.

At least they were nice enough to use the coasters, I'd thought to myself.

I grabbed the remote control from the coffee table and turned off the TV. Jinni woke up immediately as if someone had poured a bucket of water on her face, but DJ never looked up from his game.

Since Tuesday, my sister and her kids had been staying over at my house taking over the living room, the guest room, and leaving the kitchen a hot mess morning, noon, and night.

I stood over her as she looked around, half-sleep and grumpy like she had forgotten where she was.

"Jinni, why aren't the kids in school?"

She grumbled something under her breath and sat up, yawning long and hard.

"And I thought you were going back home today," I said to her, trying to keep the grave annoyance from my tone.

"Today isn't over yet," she snapped, noticing my aggravation and giving me a hint of attitude. She reached for her phone on the side table next to her, and I noticed three cigarette butts in one of my crystal bowls.

"Jinni!" I wailed.

"What?" she jumped up like she had bugs on her.

"My candy dish from Europe! Really? And you're smoking in the house?" I grabbed the crystal bowl and charged towards the kitchen to dump the ashes and cigarettes in the trash can. I squirted dish detergent on the expensive glass, washed it out vigorously, and then set it on the counter.

"You didn't have any aluminum foil so I had to use what I could."

"I said no smoking in the house, Jinni! I hate the smell. Use the balcony!"

"You don't have anywhere to sit out there!"

"I don't care!"

The kids gawked at me; even DJ tore his eyes away from his game to look. I took a deep breath and said calmly, "I don't want my place smelling like a pool hall."

"Relax. I cracked the window and sprayed air freshener."

Relax?

My blood started to boil. Jinni shook her head, her short bob swinging like a pendulum. I gave her the meanest glare I could muster before going into my room and slamming the door. I tossed my purse on my bed and even though I didn't hear my phone send a text alert, I checked it anyway for a message from Trey.

Nothing.

Irritated, I shot a text to Jinni. **Please be gone by eight.**

Seconds later, I could hear her feet shuffling towards my bedroom door.

Knock. Knock.

"Jinni, go away."

The door let out a sighing creak as she turned the doorknob and opened it. "Can I come in?"

"No," I told her, but Jinni moseyed her ass on in any way. I clinched the side of my head. It felt like a headache was starting to happen.

"Jinni, get out. I don't feel like talking."

She closed the door behind her and stepped further into my bedroom. "Just let me apologize. I was angry when I called you a home-wrecker."

"You didn't call me a home-wrecker."

Her face fell. "Oh... well, I guess I didn't say it, but I thought it."

"Jin!"

"Okay, okay! I'm sorry for all those other things I said. And the smoking-"

"Jinni, when are you leaving?" I quipped, cutting her off. "You've been here for days. I love you guys, but I'm going through some stuff too and I need to be alone in my space."

The sincere look in her eyes faded fast and she glared at me. "Did you not hear me when I said I'm going through a divorce?" she hissed.

"I heard you loud and clear."

"What am I supposed to do?" she asked, her eyes begging me for answers.

"Jinni, there's always a silver lining to every cloud," I soothed. Her brow wrinkled.

"What the hell are you talking about?"

"I'm saying, you will get over this. This too shall pass. A problem is a chance for you to do your best."

"I'm being fuckin' serious and you're quoting Duke Ellington?"

"I'm being serious too." I pulled out of my blazer and went inside my walk-in closet to hang it up. "I know this is hard and you're probably embarrassed, but I think you will benefit from telling your side of the story. In fact, Lo is looking for an exclusive. This would be perfect."

"Airing my dirty laundry?" Jinni quipped.

"Honey, your dirty laundry is already out on the clothesline in the front yard for all to see. The world knows about Donovan and how he can't keep his dick in his pants. But no one has heard from you—his wife. You've let this shit go on long enough. Speaking out about the divorce and what you went through will be an inspiration for women who aren't strong enough to make that move."

Jinni looked paralyzed with fear. "I can't do that."

"You can. Jinni, you are strong and brave. Well, at least the Jinni I knew growing up. You didn't take shit from anybody. You can't keep taking this shit from Donovan."

"The kids... I'm not ready."

"I know. And they probably won't understand but trust me they will once they get older. The girls will look up to you for walking away from a relationship like this. You don't want them to think being in a toxic relationship is right, Jinni."

Jinni pulled at her hair. Her blunt-cut wig was tossed to the side. Her real hair was a ratty bird's nest on top of her head.

"I don't know if I'm ready to put myself out there like

that. I hired a private investigator. I want to know who this woman is."

"I'm dying to know who this woman is too. I mean, if it's a woman."

Jinni glared at me. I laughed.

"I'm teasing. Of course, it's a woman. And when you find out who she is, let us know. Maybe we can get her a two-page spread. His mistress may be keeping her lips sealed now, but they can't keep this hidden forever. Donavon is too big of a star."

My phone began to ring. I disappeared into my master bathroom, letting Jinni contemplate. Trey's name flashed across the screen and like always, my heart fluttered. I shut the door to the bathroom for privacy and leaned against the sink.

"Hi," I answered breathlessly.

"Hey! I needed to hear your voice before I stepped into this meeting."

My cheeks grew warm and a smile tugged at the corner of my lips. "How sweet."

"Are you still picking me up from the airport Friday?"

"Yeah, of course. I got you."

"This sounds cheesy, but I can't stop thinking about you," he cooed.

My smile grew to my ears by then. But like a dark cloud moving fast through a smoky sky, my mood shifted. My throat tightened and I got nervous, afraid to voice the question that had been bouncing around in my head since I left my girlfriends at the Sea Bar. "Um, I just... I need to ask you something."

"Okay, what's wrong?"

"Were you dating her while you were with me?" I'd said it fast, like ripping a band-aid off a wound. Once it was out, I was on the edge, waiting for his answer. It took Trey a minute to respond as if he didn't understand the question or maybe he forgot who "*her*" was since he'd been spending all his waking moments with me.

"What? Oh! Goodness Marley, no," Trey replied. "Seriously?" He'd sounded offended.

"I mean, your reason for breaking up with me never made sense."

"That's because I didn't know how to word it," he flustered. He groaned; I could tell it was a groan that time. A groan filled with annoyance. "I thought we'd talk about this when I got back-"

"Why do we have to talk about it when you get back? What's wrong with talking about it right now?" I blurted out; my anger started to settle in.

"Because I want you to see the seriousness in my eyes when I tell you how sorry I am. So, you can believe me when I tell you that leaving you was a mistake."

I was so filled with emotion that I could barely breathe. "You're right! You shouldn't have left me. But you did and for what?"

My mind drifted back to the day Trey had broken up with me. I'd been super excited about something, I forget now, but he'd shattered my high with his words of despair.

I remember the solemn expression on his face, and how he nervously shuffled his weight from one leg to the other looking like a little boy trying to remember his Easter speech.

My happiness dimmed and worry consumed me. The way Trey was looking and carrying on, I thought someone had died. I never thought his next words would be, "this relationship isn't working for me."

The word "what" fell from my mouth as if I didn't hear him correctly. And Trey went on, never repeating himself but telling me how much he adored me and that with time he could be the man I needed, but he just couldn't do it right now. A more traumatized and puzzled "what" escaped me, along with a heavy stream of tears. I seemed frozen, stuck in place, but my eyes moved fast, searching his own to see if it was all a joke. Trey looked away from me and I grew more frantic. "Trey!" I hollered to get his attention. It was like someone else had morphed inside of his body, talking for him, moving his hands that couldn't stop shuffling through his dirty blonde hair. His startling blue eyes were even sadder when he met my gaze again. It was then I knew Trey was for real. He was breaking up with me.

Trey had never given me a solid answer then and I waited for him to give me one now. I listened on the other end of the phone as he sighed and started sentences, he couldn't finish. The more he hesitated, the more I became.

"Damn it, Trey. Just spit it out! You're dating a white woman now. Is that what this is all about? Is this why I never met your mother? Am I too *black* for her? Are you ashamed of me?" I argued.

"Wow," Trey exhaled. He scoffed. "Look, Marley, this is too OD for me. Call me when you chill out."

The call ended before I could say anything else.

YOU

7

Friday, October 6

Dating outside our race was something new for Trey and me. We met online but told everyone we met at the Telfair Museum. When I came across his picture, I'd almost thought it was a photo of Paul Walker. My thumb hovered over Trey's photo and I hesitated on whether I should swipe right to show him I was interested or swipe left and let him continue being a stranger. I was shocked in that moment at how bad I wanted to get to know him. I had to see those icy blue eyes and sandy brown hair in person. But surely this man claiming to be a dog walker while attending law school had no interest in a black woman sporting a natural fro with skin as brown as a milk chocolate Godiva truffle.

I read over Trey's profile again and again and finally

figured I had nothing to lose. My heart raced when I saw the confetti explode across my screen, indicating that we were a match. I beamed and wrote him immediately, our conversation a flirtatious banter until he asked to meet me for drinks later that night.

Trey and I were inseparable after our first date. He'd never mentioned my skin color or said things like, "you're pretty for a black girl" that night or any time after. In fact, Trey never questioned my race or how I looked. In all those months we'd been together, we had always talked openly about everything black and white. It had never been an issue or uncomfortable. I fell for him and I didn't see color, so I was extremely irritated with myself when I'd pulled out the race card and slammed it down on our relationship. I felt ashamed of myself.

The more I festered over it, the more I wondered did I even really need an explanation? He ditched me! And it shouldn't matter why? I should move on.

Those were my thoughts when I waited at the terminal for him, my arms crossed tightly in front of me. The Savannah airport was hardly ever packed, but today there were all kinds of tourists and locals boarding and disembarking planes for their business or pleasure trips.

When Trey exited the gate pulling a carry-on suitcase and holding a messenger bag over his shoulder, a flurry of wildness started to dance inside me. The look on his face was soothing and his woodsy cologne enveloped me when he wrapped his arms around me, giving me a long firm hug. I felt his lips kiss the top of my head and feeling slightly embarrassed, I pulled away. We hadn't talked much since I accused him of dumping me for being black. It was an absurd accusation, I realized later, but I couldn't take the words back.

Trey walked close beside me. He told me he didn't have any bags at the terminal so we exited the airport and I led him to my car. We drove in silence for five minutes before he grabbed my hand and gave it a gentle squeeze.

"I missed you," he said and cracked a sideways grin. The smile alone was enough to warm me up inside and I smiled too.

"I'm sorry for what I said," I told him, suddenly feeling foolish.

"Don't apologize."

I'd kept my focus on the road, but I could feel Trey's eyes burning into the right side of my face. "I understand why you would think that. But I want you to know that that is not the case. At all. My mother knows all about you, Marley. And I know this sounds hella lame, but her best friend is black. It has nothing to do with my mother. She's just a hard woman to please. I've never introduced her to any of my girlfriends."

Trey pauses as if wondering should he let the conversation rest here or should he tell me everything. "And... you're right about me not being completely honest with you."

"Oh?" I gripped the steering wheel tighter. My ears were perked, waiting for Trey to confess that our relationship had been a lie. That he'd been cheating on me for...

well, I don't know how long in our relationship, but cheating, nonetheless.

I started to feel sick to my stomach. I didn't want Trey telling me anything that would make me hate him or make me never want to talk to him again. I wasn't ready to face the truth.

Trey opened his mouth to say more, but I cut him off, blurting out the first thing I could think to say. "You can't come to my house."

"Why? What's wrong?" he asked.

"Jinni. She and the kids are still camping out there."

"Oh yeah," he said remembering what I'd told him a couple of days ago. "It's no problem. We can go to my place."

"Your place?" I questioned with surprise. I took my eyes off the road to see if he was serious.

"Yeah, my apartment. There's more privacy there. No kids. No siblings," he flirted.

How about no fiancée?

Trey saw the skepticism on my face. He was reading my thoughts.

"All of that is over now." He'd said it without remorse. He didn't sound bitter or angry. He didn't look heartbroken. A piece of me felt relieved.

I exhaled. "What happened?"

"You," Trey answered simply.

With Trey, it never took long for me to lose my self-control. The way he held me kissed me; I could never contain myself. I watched his head bob between my thighs, his tongue gliding on my clit to the smooth lyrics of Maxwell. My fingers clenched his bedroom sheets in hopes to gain control of the orgasm I felt was coming on too strong. I could feel it rising up and through me so hard, my body started to shiver. I called his name out loud, gripping his silky black hair in my hands. Like a volcano, I erupted and called out to God and his son. Trey keeps going, licking me like a lion slurping water in a stream until I can barely contain myself.

My fingernails pierced through his sheets as a wave of ecstasy took over and gushed out of me. A sensuous scream exploded from my mouth. My body went limp. Trey lifted his head from between my legs and looked at me with a satisfied grin. His lips were glossy from my love juice. I tried to catch my breath as he climbed up my body and spooned me from behind. My staggered breathing sent us both in a fit of laughter.

"Ohmigod!" I sighed wildly.

"I love making you scream my name," he moaned. He caressed my thighs and then pulled my hair from my face. "Did you know you can speak in tongues?"

I slapped his arm. "Shut up. I do not!"

"You do. It's so cute."

We laughed again, and it melted into a comfortable silence. We rested together, with no words, just the sounds of our uneven breathing. It's almost five o'clock. I still have time to go home and get ready for Gia's party. The thought of Jinni and her kid's still lodging at my house makes me snuggle closer to Trey. I don't want to leave here.

"What are your plans for the rest of the day?" I asked him.

He sighed roughly. "Well, besides the gym, I'm going to dinner later with Johnny Jameson."

I repeated the name as if that would help me remember. It sounded oddly familiar, but when I recognized it as the most infamous lawyer in the state of Georgia, I nearly leaped out of bed. "Wait, thee Johnny Jameson from The Jameson Firm?" I squealed with excitement.

Trey laughed. "Yes."

I straddled him and cupped his face in my hands. "Johnny Jameson! What does this mean, Trey? Are you going to be working with him?"

Johnny Jameson was a household name. He'd been an attorney for just about every A-list celebrity you could think of. He was known for making you walk free no matter what you were up against. His case with RJ Givens, an actor who many believed killed his wife, was viewed all over the world. Johnny worked the case flawlessly, and RJ thanked his lucky stars all the way out of the courtroom when he was surprisingly found not guilty. The case elevated Johnny to become the most sought-after attorney on the globe.

Trey shrugged and nodded and at the same time,

tried to play modestly. Hopefully, I have a good enough resume, and he falls for my charismatic personality."

"Stop it! You know you have all of that and then some. I can't believe this. Do you know how hard it is to get an interview with Johnny Jameson?"

"You're asking me," he replied sarcastically.

"This is amazing! You've been working your ass off and now look at you!"

Trey smiled proudly.

"We should celebrate right after your dinner," I said.

"I thought you had some event to go to tonight?"

"I'll leave early. We can get drinks and come back here for a nightcap."

"Sounds like a plan," he said and tucked a strand of hair behind my ear. I pushed him in his chest. "How am I more excited about this than you?" I asked in awe.

Trey grinned, a twinkle in his eye. "I think I'm more excited at seeing you excited."

I stood over him; my feet sank into his plush mattress. "I'm super excited!" I exclaimed and started hopping up and down. Trey bounced under me, laughing at my childish behavior. When he couldn't take it anymore, he grabbed my ankles and gave them a gentle pull. I dropped down on top of him, my naked body sitting on his lower stomach. I felt his dick jump against my ass.

Trey stared deep into my eyes. He had a way of looking at me like no one else mattered. It was a look we gave each other often, where no words needed to be said because we both knew how deeply we felt about one another. If Lo and Harper could see how Trey and I were alone, maybe they would understand. Maybe they could see how he would come back to me. It was a mistake and I forgave him.

I kissed his lips, and he pushed his tongue into my mouth. I could taste myself on him. My cum still glazed around his mouth. I gasped when his dick slid into me. He loved me slow and then faster, taking my mind, body, and soul to cloud nine.

FAMILIAR

8

Friday, October 6

Gia's birthday party took place at her sleek, contemporary mansion in a well-hidden suburb on the islands. There was a valet service in the front yard and a wait staff waiting on guests' hand and foot. The house and backyard were decorated in every shade of pink you could think of, with pops of gold and silver throughout.

All of Hip-Hop royalty was in attendance, dancing, and mingling, living their best life. A videographer was present taping the event's spectacular moments. There were also two photographers capturing pictures. One of the photographers gathered Gia, Lo, Harper, and me together, directing us on where to stand. The four of us snaked our arms around each other's waist and posed. We were dressed to impress in our glamorous ensembles, but

Gia stole the show in her custom nude gown bedazzled with diamonds and pearls.

"Beautiful," the photographer exclaimed. "Show me those sexy smiles!" The four of us laughed and smiled as the flash went off.

The DJ who was set up on an elaborate booth near Gia's resort-style pool filled with floating pool lights played Gia's latest single and the party went wild. Gia jumped with glee and we danced with her to her new hit song. When it was over Lyle's voice boomed through a standing microphone only to startle the celebration. "Excuse me, everyone!"

The DJ faded the music until all we could hear was Lyle clicking a silver spoon against his whiskey glass. "Can I have everyone's attention please," he asked lightly. When all eyes seemed to be on him, Lyle grinned affectedly. He wasn't a knock-out, but he was cute. He looked distinguished in his black tuxedo pants and matching vest and tie. "I'd like to make a toast to the birthday girl. My wife." His eyes wandered the scene looking for his high school sweetheart. Gia blushed as Harper nudged her from our circle out into the open. Gia gave her a playful side-eye.

"Ah, there she is. Come here, baby," Lyle called out to her.

Gia lifted the hem of her dress as she seemed to glide towards Lyle who stood in front of the DJ booth. They joined hands and Lyle gave her a soft peck on the cheek, making Gia's cheeks more crimson

"Let's make a toast!" Lyle waved over a curvy woman

serving the night's signature drink. A pink concoction of mixed alcohol with a puff of pink cotton candy hanging on the side of the glass. "A Frenchy," the waitress had called it. Lyle handed a glass to Gia and then raised his own in the air.

"Gia, baby, I hope you're having the time of your life tonight. You deserve all of this and more. Nothing brings me as much happiness as you do, baby. I love you so much."

"Awww," voices cooed in unison.

"To Gia," Lyle cheered. Glasses clinked and people cheered and saluted Gia on her special day, shouting out all kinds of congratulations in her honor. Gia laughed, hiding her blushing face in the crook of Lyle's arm. She raised her glass and then turned to kiss Lyle. It was a kiss so long and sexy I had to look away. Lo and I exchanged glances and laughed. The applauds got louder and the DJ started the music up again, playing an old-school jam by Mystical.

Gia went wild and sashayed her ass to the dance floor which was strategically placed next to the pool. She popped her infamous twerk move and showed us that even at the ripe age of 35 she could still drop it low. Her guests exploded into a cheerful uproar when her husband Lyle joined in. He stood from behind, grabbing her hip with one hand and raising the roof with the other. The two of them moved in sync, dirty dancing as Nivea's voice took over the hook, singing *"been so looooong, he's been onnnn. So please, show me, what it is that you wanna see"*.

The two looked so happy and in love which made me think of Trey and his meeting with Johnny Jameson. I looked down at my phone. No call. No text.

"That's like the fifth time in three minutes you've looked at your phone," Lo observed.

"Oh. Yeah, sorry. I'm expecting a call." I said, not meaning to look at my phone again.

"From Trey?" she asked. His name seemed to alert Harper whose two-step turned into an off-beat shimmy. She turned her eyes from Gia and Lyle and looked at Lo and me. "Trey? What about him?" she asked.

"He's on an interview slash dinner with Johnny Jameson right now," I revealed.

Harper raised an eyebrow. "That's a big deal."

"Yeah," Lo added with less enthusiasm.

"Wait? Jameson? Why does that name sound familiar?" Harper asked, snapping her fingers to the beat.

"He's a big-time lawyer!" I answered in disbelief.

Harper rolled her eyes. "Well duh, I know who he is."

"So, I guess things are really over with Trey and his fiancée," Lo peered at me over her glass. "I'm glad you two figured everything out."

I gave her a look. "Are you really?"

"Of course!" she exclaimed, scoffing at the frown on my face. "I mean, I think it's weird. And I can only imagine how their break-up ended. Time and money wasted, plus all that planning for nothing."

"Nothing?" I snapped. "So, my relationship with Trey has boiled down to nothing."

Harper danced off in another direction. Lo caught wind of her slip up and winced.

"Okay, that came out all wrong."

"You're good." My glass was empty, so I used that as an excuse to escape from the ridicule.

I entered the house, which was just as crowded and lively as the backyard. I wanted to escape the noise and bustle, but a husky security guard was standing on the bottom step, blocking people from heading up to Gia and Lyle's personal quarters. I sighed and headed towards the guest bathroom they had downstairs. There was a line of seven people waiting to use it.

I sent Trey a text message. How's it going?

"You would think a house this big would have more than one bathroom for us to use?" A masculine voice from behind me said. I turned and looked up at the most handsome man I'd ever seen. My mouth parted with a sigh as he smiled down at me with eyes so brown and alluring.

"Um-yeah-well, they have a bathroom on the other end too," I stammered.

And one outside in the guest house, but I didn't mention it. I just stared, trying not to drool as I looked him over.

The top three buttons on his oxford shirt were casually undone. In his free hand, he held a highball, three-quarters full of cognac-colored liquor and cubes of ice. His skin didn't seem real. So smooth and so dark, like mocha beans. A piece of me wanted to reach out and caress his cheek with the back of my hand. I could tell he put in work at the gym by the way his navy-blue dinner jacket covered his masculine arms.

"Guess I didn't see it," he answered with that stunning grin. "You know, I'm not even going to lie to you. I came over because I wanted to talk to you." This fine-ass man had the nerve to look bashful. He laughed nervously. That made my heart melt even more. He was a humble, fine-ass man.

"I'm Othello Kingston," he offered and extended a strong and rather large hand.

"Hi," I took his hand in mine, not wanting to let it go. His grip was firm and I tried to tackle the emotions soaring around inside of me. I didn't understand it. The fluttering in my stomach felt like turbulence on a plane. "Marley Jacobs," I told him. A bell rang in my head and my smile grew wider. "Wait a minute. Othello Kingston? I read your book about racism and systematic oppression." I snapped my fingers as if it would help me remember the title. "*Unapologetic*," I guessed after a beat.

"Yes, that would be me," he said awe-stricken. "I can't believe you read my work".

"Who hasn't? It was a New York Times best-seller. And not to mention it was featured in Mod Magazine last year."

"Okay, now I'm starting to get scared," he teased.

I laughed. "Don't be. I'm editor-in-chief of Mod."

"Wow, OK. That's what's up! You know I want to thank you. I think the exposure from Mod helped a lot."

"I wouldn't give us all the credit. You're a brilliant writer."

Othello looked at me with peaked interest. There was a delayed pause, the intensity between us building. Something about his energy grabbed me, putting me in a trance.

"Are you here for Gia or Lyle?" he asked.

"Gia. We went to college together."

"Oh, word? You went to Howard too? I don't remember seeing you around. I hung out with Lyle. And Lyle and Gia-

"-were always together," we finished together and then bent over with laughter.

"That's so true, but Gia and I were into different things in college so we weren't together a lot. I didn't stay on campus either."

"Maybe so. I definitely would have remembered a girl like you," he said.

Again. Another lost in each other's eyes moment.

Othello's lips started to speak at the same time my phone rang. Trey. And for some odd reason, I felt exposed. I didn't know what to say as I looked at Othello and then back at my phone. The shrill ring tone rattled my guilty conscience.

I winced. "I'm so sorry. I have to take this," I told Othello. I moved out of the line and back into the crowded living room to take the call. It was way too noisy so I weaved through the crowd of the rich and famous and exited out the front door.

"Trey," I gushed. "How did it go?"

"It went very well. I start next week," he boasted.

I squealed in delight, listening to him laugh with joy on the other end.

"That's amazing, Trey! How do you feel?"

"I feel unstoppable! I don't think it's going to hit me yet until I walk through those doors and sit at my new desk in my new corner office."

I was grinning so hard my cheeks hurt. "We have to celebrate."

"Yes, we do. I'm just leaving from here. I can meet you at my place in thirty minutes."

"Make it forty. I'm going to stop and get champagne."

"OK, baby," he purred.

My fist clenched with excitement. I was just about to rush inside to spill the good news to my girls, but Lo and Harper were already stepping out the front door into the cool night air. Their faces looked troublesome. "What's wrong with y'all?" I asked.

Harper pinched her lips together.

"Just show her," Lo insisted.

Harper looked down at her phone and then thrust it towards me. Her screen was on someone's Instagram page, and I instantly realized it was her Instagram page. Alyssa Jameson. Her latest picture was posted 12 hours ago—a photo of Trey on one knee, holding a diamond ring. Alyssa stands in front of him, wearing the most stunning slip dress, her hands covering her surprised expression and a thousand-watt smile. The caption underneath reading, *reminiscing on the night I said, Hell Yes! Can't wait to spend forever with you, Trey Nicholas Ellis.*

I looked up to Lo and Harper and all they did was nod solemnly. "This was posted 12 hours ago," I told them as if they didn't already know.

"Exactly," Harper said. "And Johnny Jameson is her dad!"

JAM

9

Saturday, October 6

I left the party in a blind rage. Tears of anger blurred my vision. I drove straight to Trey's house, ready for answers to the questions I'd purposely avoided.

Once I made it into the city, I decided to skip a drive full of Abercorn stoplights and merge onto Truman Parkway. The things I wanted to know and say couldn't wait much longer. Taking the highway would get me to his house faster. Or so I thought. As soon as I merged onto Truman I drove into a traffic jam. I slammed my hand on the steering wheel. The only reason for bumper-to-bumper traffic on Truman is because of an accident.

My car came to a complete stop. I cursed under my breath. I could feel my anxiety swelling up inside of me just as the ringing of my cell echoed through the speakers in my car. I pressed the talk button on my steering wheel to answer it.

"Hey, Marley. Just checking up on you." Lo's sincere voice resonated inside the car.

"I'll be okay. I'm just..." I sighed, too exhausted to finish. I shook my head, the tears that were welling up in my eyes finally falling down my cheeks. "I feel so stupid. I believed him."

"You're human. Shit like this happens all the time with men like him."

"I should have known better," I whimpered. "I'm smarter than this!"

"Marley! Don't be so hard on yourself. It's ok!"

"It's not ok. I did a fuckin' retreat to get this man out of my system," I scoffed at the thought.

"It wasn't just for him, Marley. It was for you too. You were stressed with work and had no time for self-care. You needed that retreat for you. We're not going to give that bastard all the credit."

"I should have asked more questions," I said to myself.

"So, you guys never talked?" Lo asked me.

"Not like we should have. I never pressed the issue. I was just..." my voice fades to silence.

"Damn, Marley. You need to talk to him."

"Oh, trust me. I plan to get some answers tonight."

The car in front of me inched forward and I followed suit. An ambulance whizzed past, the sirens so loud, I winced. The earsplitting warning drowned out the end of Lo's sentence, and I had to tell her to repeat herself.

"I said... it's best you get some closure from this clown and then move on!"

"I know. I guess I wasn't ready for closure, but I'm more confused now than when I found out he was engaged."

"Right! Johnny Jameson's daughter? That's crazy!"

"I just don't get it. How did they meet? When did they meet? He's such an introvert. And she's so..."

Gorgeous.

"Famous?" Lo questioned.

"Well, yeah, but she's not in the limelight compared to her Trey is pretty much a nobody."

"Exactly. He's a nobody! This is why it shouldn't be so hard for you to break up with him. Tonight," Lo stressed.

I felt a little pull on my heartstrings when she said that.

"And you have to end this with him, Marley. It's for your own good. Don't fall for any more of his bullshit. I swear, it's like he's got you under some weird-ass spell."

"He doesn't have me under anything," I blurted. "I just simply let my guard down. Despite the retreat and despite what I knew in my gut, I was lonely, and I used Trey to fill that void. I'm not gonna blame this on him."

"Wow. Deep," Lo sighed. "Keep that in the back of your mind when you're breaking up with his ass."

"I'm going to tell him..." I couldn't finish. My car was finally close enough to view the accident. And even though the sky was dark, the blaring lights from the cars and ambulance gave me a clear view of what was holding up traffic. The silver vehicle in the median wouldn't have made my eyes bug out if it hadn't been for the tag number I knew so well. It seemed to be the only thing intact as the rest of the car was crushed and destroyed. A tow truck reeled Trey's car in slow motion on the bed of his truck. Everything was a dented mess.

My heart dropped like a flash of lightning. I felt faint. I watched the paramedics lift the stretcher with Trey's bloody body on it, pushing it through the grass and rushing him to the ambulance.

"Marley," Lo called. I watched in horror as the medics jumped inside the back of the truck with Trey, slammed the doors shut, and then raced off towards Memorial hospital.

"You're going to tell him what?" she hollered.

"Ohmigod, Lo. It's Trey!" I screamed.

MOMMY

10

Saturday, October 6

My head was pounding with tension when Lo and Harper made it to the ER. I stopped my frantic pacing just enough to rush into Lo's outstretched arms. She held me tight, rubbing my back. Only then did my worry start to settle.

Harper stood aside; her arms crossed in front of her. "I'm here for you. Not him," she yapped.

"What did the doctors say?" Lo asked, rolling her eyes.

"He's in ICU, but he's stable. A few broken bones." I pushed my hair back from my forehead and sighed. "I thought he was dead."

Lo gave my shoulder a reassuring squeeze.

"This may be the wrong time to say this, but I hope

you still plan on breaking things off with him. This little stunt doesn't change anything," Harper quipped.

Lo, and I gave her an awkward stare. Harper held her hands up in defense and then turned and walked away.

"Does he know you're here?"

I pinched the bridge of my nose. "He's not awake yet."

"I'm sure he'll be fine. Come on. I rode with Harper, but I'll drive you home in your car."

My eyes stretched with panic. "No, Lo. I can't leave. Trey is going to need someone here when he wakes up."

Lo looked at me as if I'd lost my mind. "Girl, you can't stay here! Trey is clearly still engaged. He's got a whole fiancée. I'm sure she's going to be bursting through these doors any minute."

"You're right," I said sadly. The ache in my belly made me nauseous. I'd forgotten about Alyssa.

"We'll wait here."

I drifted back to the elevator and rode up to the ICU unit, shuffling my feet as I picked apart the lies Trey told me. Why was he willing to celebrate something so pivotal as getting a new job with me instead of her?

I drowned out the ominous thoughts swimming in my mind when I reached Trey's room and saw a heavy-set white woman standing by his bedside. Her shoulders were jerking and she was crying. Her words were inaudible as she spoke over Trey's comatose body. My jacket and purse were laying on the opposite side of his bed in a chair, but I stood there, frozen and unsure of what to do next.

I cleared my throat to get the woman's attention, not wanting to walk in and startle her. But somehow, I still managed to spook her because she turned and looked at me like I was a ghost. Her face settled. "Marley," she uttered.

I nodded. "Yes. I'm sorry, who are you?"

"I'm Mrs. Ellis. Trey's mother." The coldness in her voice left me stunned.

I studied her face, marking the resemblance she and her only child shared. The same sharp nose. The same penetrating eyes. Trey had never spoken much about his parents only that his father had passed away when he was ten and his mother had pretty much been a loner and single ever since. If she was this intense with everyone, then I could see why.

"What are you doing here?" she asked, her face twisted in confusion.

"I saw the accident. I wanted to make sure he was okay."

"You saw it? What happened?" Her voice was stern and sharp.

"I'm not sure. I wasn't there when it actually happened. I pulled up right after…"

Mrs. Ellis held her hand up to stop my rambling. "I don't understand," she cringed. "You were there? Now you're here. Didn't Trey break up with you? Are you stalking my son?"

"The last thing I'd be doing is stalking your son," I snapped.

"Trey doesn't need any ex-girlfriends as friends,"

Mrs. Ellis spat the word friends out like it was a curse. "He's getting married. You are aware of that, aren't you?"

"No, I wasn't aware. In fact, I'm confused, because Trey and I have been spending an awful amount of time together these past few weeks."

The dire look on her face melted into despair. "What do you mean?"

"I mean I was under the intentions that he and I were back together. Maybe he didn't tell her yet."

She walked up to me, her stare menacingly. "You're lying."

When I didn't say anything she chortled. "He wouldn't put what he has with Jameson in jeopardy. Not for some fling."

"Excuse me, I dated your son for a year. It wasn't a fling then and it's not a fling now."

"Did you give him some ultimatum? What kind of game are you playing? Coming up with vicious lies to ruin what I've worked so hard for."

"I don't know what Trey told you, but-"

"You need to leave! The last thing I need is you messing this up for us? Because if Trey finds this little episode is the reason they changed their minds on making him partner, he will never forgive you."

"Me?" I questioned Mrs. Ellis in amazement. "I would be the reason they changed their mind? I'm not the one plotting and scheming to get a job Trey is capable of getting on his own. Did you seriously pimp your son out to get a job with Jameson?"

Mrs. Ellis flinched and her hand went to her chest as

if she would have a heart attack at any moment. I looked at her in disgust. "You know, for weeks I thought Trey broke up with me because I was a black woman, but it's you; controlling his life as if he isn't talented or smart enough to work for a company like that."

"What the hell are you talking about? You don't think I know what my son is capable of?! It's all about connections. Sometimes it's who you know that can get you ahead in life."

"Is that what you call it? Meanwhile, people's feelings are getting strung along at your expense. Does Alyssa know you two used her to get this job?"

A sinister smile spread across Mrs. Ellis' fuchsia-painted lips. "You really have no idea, do you?" Her face seemed to draw closer to mine. "I will take full responsibility for arranging the dinner for my son to meet Johnny. I saw a chance and I took it! But that's all I did. I never set up anything with Alyssa and Trey. You'll have to blame chemistry on that, sweetie."

At that point, I wanted to walk away. Everything in me fought to leave, but I stood there. My feet felt like they'd been nailed to the floor, unable to move. Ms. Ellis inched close and closer into my personal space.

"I didn't know Johnny would bring his wife and daughter to the dinner I set up, but he did. And you'd have to be blind not to see the way my son's eyes lit up when he saw Alyssa walk into the room. My son was mesmerized. Sparks were flying between them from the moment they laid eyes on each other. So, no, I didn't force Trey to do anything he didn't want to do. Trey fell in love, on his own. No help from mommy."

It took all that I had not to lash out. All that I had not to fold, and all that I had not to put my hands around Mrs. Ellis' wrinkled, rubbery neck. I had plenty of bail money, but I didn't need a case. I grabbed my things from the chair and charged out of the room.

Everything that old woman said made sense. But was that really how Trey and Alyssa met or was she just fucking with me? It was clear she didn't like me. She could have been saying anything to get me out of that room. Trey found the right time to be present but unable to explain himself. Nothing he said would have mattered anyway. I was done.

I was so focused on what happened that I nearly crashed into Alyssa during my exit. The two of us stopped firmly in our tracks. She smiled an apology, but once her eyes roamed over my face, the smile vanished. She looked jarred, and I wondered if she knew of me, just like I knew of her.

"Excuse me," I said out of habit. I moved around her and onto the elevator. Alyssa looked down the hall at Trey's room door but the doors to the elevator were already closing when her eyes shot back at me. She gasped.

Yeah, Alyssa Jameson knew exactly who I was.

SWIPE

11

Friday, October 19

Yoga had become my new favorite thing to do. An active way of relaxing my mind, and bringing myself to a place of calmness. I started going every day of the week to a cute little studio in midtown and I always left feeling more focused, energized, and invigorated.

Today the weather was amazingly cool, so the owner held the yoga session on the lush green grass of Forsyth park under the sun. It was *"bring a friend for free"* day so I brought along Lo who was struggling to keep up. When it was over Lo collapsed on her mat, face to the sky, her chest heaving up and down.

"You do this every day?" she asked, her breathing choppy.

"Yes," I laughed. I sat down on my mat next to her

and took a swig from my water bottle. Other yogis were leaving or standing nearby making small talk.

"I feel like I'm going to die. I thought this was a therapeutic exercise?" Lo admitted.

"It's your first time. You'll get used to it."

I laid down and looked up at the sky. The clouds were so big and full, contorted into whimsical shapes. I imagined myself floating away on one of them, whisking myself off to an island far *far* away.

"You ever thought about how far the clouds travel before they melt away?" I asked.

Lo turned her head to look at me. "Are you high?"

"No."

"Hmph."

"I think I need a change of scenery. I wouldn't mind moving to Chicago or New York."

"Take a vacation. You don't need to move. I can't have my best friend living miles away from me."

"We take flights all the time. What would be different? Plus, I feel like I need to get away from Savannah."

"Get away from Savannah or get away from Trey."

I scoffed. "*Savannah*."

"How's he doing by the way?"

I closed my eyes and propped my arm over my forehead. "I don't know. I called a couple of days after the accident and they said he was discharged. Haven't heard anything else. The fact that he hasn't tried to call me tells me everything I need to know."

"What are you going to do if you move?" Lo asked.

"Same thing I do in Savannah. Write. New York has some amazing publishing companies."

"I don't have anything against you moving and doing bigger and better things, but don't let this baggage you've got with Trey be the reason you're moving your life somewhere else."

"I told you it has nothing to do with Trey."

"Did you forget I've known you since we were fifteen? I *know* you, Marley. You act like you aren't phased and run away from problems you don't want to deal with."

"So what do you suggest I do?" I asked.

"Unless you want this baggage, *Trey*, to keep consuming your thoughts, you need to talk to him. Talk! Because no matter where you move he's still going to be right here." She reached over to put her index finger on the side of my head. "And then you need to stop beating yourself up about this. You aren't the only woman to give a man that didn't deserve it a second chance."

Lo did know me well because that's exactly how I felt; angry at myself for feeding my loneliness with Trey's energy. I sighed and opened my eyes to the sky again. The clouds I'd just seen were gone. There was nothing but clear blue skies.

"Once you get an understanding, you'll be able to close the door on him and the relationship."

I hoped Lo was right. I still couldn't get Ms. Ellis' words out of my head, her voice sounding like nails on a chalkboard. *"Sparks were flying between them from the moment they laid eyes on each other."*

When Trey and I met in person, had sparks flown? No. Sparks didn't fly and it didn't feel like a fairy tale, but it was real. At least to me, it was.

I heard my phone chime, so I sat up and reached for it at the end of my mat. Had I known it was a Hooked alert and not a text I would have kept it there. The dating app I'd downloaded out of pure boredom notified me that I had a new match. Some guy with a great smile and a full beard.

"Are you dating?" Lo asked. She was peeping over my shoulder.

"No," I sighed. "It's been nothing but pointless conversations."

"Show me your potentials?" She scooted closer as I scrolled through the guys in my messages. "Nice. Nice. And you don't like any of them?" she asked unconvincingly.

"None." I was embarrassed to even be back on this damn thing. The site was like a brochure of suitors, allowing you to cart the potentials you wanted to make time for. So shallow and unromantic.

Lo took the cell from my fingers and went to the home screen where a list of eligible bachelors awaited to be chosen. She swiped left on the guy who looked like he sold drugs for a living. Left on a man that looked like he could be someone's sugar daddy. The next photo was of a guy with caramel-colored skin and a nice smile.

"He's cute," she offered. She scrolled through his profile. *Works at Jesus Daily*, his profile read.

"Oh hell no!" we yelped.

Lo swiped left again and grunted. "It's a no for him too. He looks like he serves lies on a silver platter."

I couldn't help but laugh but Lo's eyes popped open on the next possible suitor. "Oh my," she gasped. "He's the one."

I looked at the familiar picture. It was him. The one who had come across my mind a time or two. Feelings I'd felt when we met started to stir up inside of me and I smiled.

"I've met him before. At Gia's party," I confessed. I admired his beautiful brown skin and Colgate commercial smile. His profile name read *LaidBackGuy85*, but I knew his real name was Othello.

"Wait. What?!" Lo asked in pure shock.

I snickered. "Yes, I mean I was interrupted, but we talked while we waited in line for the bathroom."

"Girl, swipe right," she pushed eagerly.

I swiped but nothing happened. No fireworks to say we were a match or to let me know that Othello was interested in me too.

Lo frowned. "Maybe he hasn't seen your profile yet."

"Maybe," I murmured.

My phone chimed again. A text from Jinni. She'd moved back home two weeks ago by order of her kids. They were tired of being stuck at my house. They wanted to play with their friends and their PlayStation, and according to Everley "my house was too small". They missed their big rooms and all the space.

Reluctantly, Jinni moved back home but was still determined to leave Donovan. I'll tell my story. Jinni's text read. I didn't know who or what encouraged Jinni to come forward and I didn't care. This would be an exclusive story and Mod would be flying off the shelf when people finally saw the wife of Donovan Sheppard on the cover. Jinni had been lurking in the shadows for years. And now that she finally had the strength to walk away from him, she would be labeled a hero and an inspiration to many.

"Lo, I think I got you a front-page article," I squealed with excitement. "Why? What happened?"

"Jinni. She's ready to come forward and tell her side of the story."

"Wow! Seriously!"

"Yeah, she said she'd do it." I turned my phone towards her to show her the text just as my phone chimed again. Lo's grin faded. "Oh wow…" she gasped.

Ding! Ding! Ding!

Text after text was coming in and with each one Lo's eyes got bigger. I turned the phone around to see what Lo was gaping at. Photos of Donovan and his mistress were being delivered to my phone back to back. The pictures were taken from afar with a quality camera that had a good zoom lens. They were the photos from the PI Jinni hired. Photos of Donovan and his mistress hugging. Photos of the two play fighting on a cobblestone street that looked like it could have been somewhere in Europe. Photos of the mistress laughing while Donovan lifted her in the air from behind. Photos of him nuzzling her neck. Photos of the mistress straddling Donovan on a beach that looked nothing like Tybee Island. The sand was too light and the water was too blue. She was topless and his hands gripped her hips as they kissed.

The pictures captured two people deeply and passionately in love, or maybe lust. It was clear that there was chemistry between them, which amazed me even more.

Donovan Sheppard had many pictures in the tabloids, but none this spicy and seductive. These images were money-shots for sure.

One thing I learned while being a journalist was that people loved a good scandal. And they were going to flip when they saw the man that was once the world's greatest point guard, with his latest conquest, neo-soul recording artist, Gia Baskins.

GONE

12

Saturday, October 19

"Ohmigod! Is this Gia?" Harper asked.

"Yes," I answered.

I watched her perfectly manicured finger slide through the photos on my phone, her head shaking in disbelief. We'd met up with her at a coffee shop right after the pictures of Gia were sent to my phone. Lo sat sipping her tea. She still looked just as dumbfounded as she did an hour ago.

"This can't be Gia."

"But it is."

"What the hell?"

"I know."

"What the hell?" Harper jabbered again, her voice in utter shock.

"I know. We can't believe it either."

"Have you talked to her yet? What did she say?"

"No. We've been calling her, but she doesn't answer. I sent a text last night. No response."

Harper looked back at the scandalous pictures on my phone again. "This has to be photoshopped."

"I wish," I sighed. "My sister had a private investigator access Gia and Donovan's phone records. They were being followed for weeks. Those proofs of them on the beach were taken in Mexico about a week ago."

"What the hell?" Harper gasped. "That was around her birthday?"

"Right."

"And now Jinni wants to air out all the dirty laundry," Lo added.

"Poor Lyle. Does he know?"

Lo shrugged miserably.

I sat there, brainstorming, thinking about Lyle and how crushed he would be when he found out the truth. For years I thought Gia and Lyle were the happiest and most secure couple ever and for months, Gia was fooling around behind his back.

"He just made that amazing toast at her birthday party," Lo thought out loud.

"Right. I just knew they would be together forever with a handful of babies," said Harper as she handed my phone back to me.

A vivid afterthought played in my memory. A grief-stricken Jinni crying and drinking away her sorrows with a bottle of champagne. Her words were angry and harsh, *"his latest hoe is pregnant!"*

"Oh wow! You guys, Gia is pregnant!"

Harper and Lo looked at me with their eyes as wide as saucers. "What?!"

"How do you know that?"

"Jinni said that Donovan's mistress is pregnant. Gia is pregnant."

Harper sunk back in her seat and buried her face in her hands.

"You're kidding me!" Lo gasped.

"I'm not."

"That explains why she's been glowing."

"And why she stopped drinking alcohol. Did any of you notice how she didn't drink after Lyle made that speech," I noted.

Lo picked up her cell. I sat there still baffled by it all.

Gia.

Pregnant.

Having an affair.

"She's still not answering the phone," Lo glowered. "What should we do?"

"We should check on Lyle."

* * *

Lyle answered the door before we had a chance to ring the doorbell. His face looked grief-stricken, masked with torment.

"Have you heard anything new?" he mumbled.

"No, nothing."

"We haven't heard a thing."

"She hasn't called us," we each admitted at the same time.

Lyle frowned and then disappeared inside his house.

We stood on the porch, glancing at each other, uncertain of what to do next until Harper boldly stepped over the threshold.

We found Lyle in the family room fixing himself a drink from a bar cart in the corner. His slowed motor skills confirmed that he'd had more than one or two.

"How are you feeling?" I asked because it was the only thing I could think to say. I immediately regretted it when Lyle peered at me like I'd asked the most ridiculous question known to man. "How am I feeling?" he scoffed. "*You* tell me. My wife is missing. How do you think I'm feeling?"

He chugged on his drink and swallowed hard.

"You don't think she'll be back?" Lo asked. "Maybe she just-"

"She's gone!" Lyle snapped. He wiped his mouth with the back of his hand. "I've already called the cops. They left about ten minutes ago." His eyes looked delirious and I instantly felt sorry for him. "They're going to do everything they can to try and find her," he mimicked.

Lyle studied us. "So, you three don't know anything? You don't know where she could have gone?"

"No," Lo shook her head. "And she won't return any of our calls."

"Her phone," I said suddenly. "You didn't track her location?"

Lyle pulled Gia's phone from his pants pocket. I knew it was hers because it was wrapped in that protective marble case she loved so much.

"She left her phone."

"Why would she leave without her phone?" I asked the question carefully, scared to strike a chord in Lyle, who already seemed to be on the verge of breaking down.

"Again. *You* tell me!" He laughed manically and shook his head. "Seems like something a woman that doesn't want to be found would do."

The three of us exchanged glances. It was obvious Lyle was in the dark about Gia and Donovan.

"Lyle, were you and Gia having any problems?" Harper asked.

He gave her an incredulous look.

"What? No! Did it look like we were having problems? She was happy! I was happy." His voice cracked. "I just don't understand. Everything was good. We were good," he lamented. "I don't understand. I just don't understand," he repeated over and over again. His balled-up fist beat the sides of his head. I wanted to give Lyle the answers to the questions he craved, but it felt like there was a ball of cotton lodged in my throat.

Our eyes followed him as he lagged back to his bar cart, found another glass, and fixed himself another cup of whiskey. "Did you know she was pregnant?" He asked casually. He watched us over the brim of his glass as he drank and waited for an answer none of us gave. "She wouldn't tell me, but I know Gia's period like the back of my hand. The throwing up and then eating everything in sight. Why was she hiding it from me?"

My heart went out to Lyle. I could feel the pain he was feeling at that moment because I had felt it at one time too. Abandonment. Betrayal. A lover leaving you in the dark with that heart-wrenching feeling of rejection.

"Lyle, Gia is having an affair," I confessed.

Tension seemed to fill the room at that moment. Lyle paused. His mouth twisted in confusion, his brow furrowed. He didn't say anything for a long time, but the tears in his eyes said it all.

"I'm so sorry," I said, my voice breaking.

Lyle nodded as if he understood and swallowed the rest of his liquor in a big gulp. "How long?"

I recalled what Jinni told me. "March."

He grunted and ruggedly swiped the tears from his cheek.

"Lyle, please know we knew nothing about this," Harper admitted.

He nodded again. Kept nodding and playing with the glass in his hands. "Who is he?" he asked.

Harper looked at me. I looked at Lo. She'd been hugging herself in the corner the whole time, her eyes watery and bouncing from one person to the next.

"I bet it's a superstar, huh? Someone with way more money than me. I guess I'm not surprised. I already knew the fame would go to her head and some shit like this would happen."

Lyle's hand gripped the glass in his hand and he squeezed it so tight I thought it would burst under pressure. He drew his arm back and threw the glass past my face and across the room. It shattered on the wall, breaking into tiny fragments on the floor. Me, Harper, and Lo jumped, our shoulders hiking up to our ears in horror.

Lyle let out a long, sad sigh. He collapsed on their leather sectional and dropped his head in his hands. "I need to be alone," he wept.

***

When I got home I called my sister. Her cell phone rang twice before she answered. "What is it?" she asked as if I was interrupting her day.

"Nothing. Just... where is Donovan?"

"He's here," Jinni snapped. "Why? Where should he be?"

I thought of Gia. "I thought..." I stopped myself. "Gia is missing. Lyle doesn't know where she is."

"And I care, because?" Jinni snarled.

"Look, I know you don't care-"

"Oh! I guess you thought her and Donovan ran off into the sunset together?"

I did, but I didn't say anything more.

"Now that you know Donovan is fucking Gia, are you going to put her on blast? Cause I don't need you changing your mind because she's your got damn friend."

"Jinni, we're doing your story-"

"But you're not going to do hers? I knew it. I fucking knew it."

"Jinni that's not what-"

"It's exactly what it is! Air her fucking business or I'll take my exclusive to someone else!"

The call ended and I looked at Lo and Harper who'd heard the entire conversation on my speaker. I wanted to scream. What the hell am I going to do? And where the hell is Gia?

HOPELESS

13

Monday, October 22

The search for Gia stopped when she called Lyle from a 718 number, letting him know she was alive and well and needed "time". He passed down the message to Harper, who delivered the message to Lo and me. We were able to breathe a little better, but that didn't stop us from worrying. When Harper tried to call the number back, a Spanish woman who spoke broken English answered the phone, having no clue what we wanted or who Gia was.

Gia had gone so far as to disconnect her phone and delete her social media pages, and someone like me knew it was to escape the wrath of angry fans who would soon be trolling her page once word got out that she'd been sleeping with a married man. I could see the headlines now. *Grammy Nominated artist, Gia Baskins, cheats on her husband with Donovan Sheppard.* Twitter was going to have a field day with this news. The world would judge her as if they themselves did no wrong.

Out of the three of us, Harper seemed to be the one feeling the most upset. She felt betrayed. She'd thought her friend since freshman year in college told her everything and she was hurt that she'd been in the dark about Gia's affair.

We discussed in my living room over Chinese takeout the when, why's and how's of Gia and Donovan's entanglement. Harper drowning her disappointment in glasses of red wine.

"Lyle had to be cheating," Harper said matter-of-factly. We were sprawled out around my coffee table on the living room floor, eating, drinking, and watching Jumping Jack Flash. Lo's pick.

"Lyle was not cheating," Lo scoffed. "Come on, think about it. Lyle? He was in love with Gia. There's no way!"

"Why? Because he was nice and loving and said all the right things," I asked bitterly, watching a scene of Whoopi Goldberg getting her sequin gown caught in a shredder.

"No. Because women cheat when they're trying to fill an emotional void," Lo answered.

An emotional void.

That's exactly what I was trying to fill when I invited Trey back into my life... and in my bed. For days I'd been feeling so detached. Walking and moving like a zombie with no feelings, and I couldn't stand it. It was my own fault for feeling so enamored by the thought of Trey and me getting back together that I was oblivious to the fact that he was having cold feet.

I saw their wedding photo on Instagram. Trey looked dapper in his ebony black evening tailcoat. His vest, wing-collared shirt, and bow-tie were as white as snow, and the smile on his face... genuine. It was said that the "lovely couple" ditched their winter wedding plans and got married right away after Trey's near-death experience.

"A penny for your thoughts. You good over there?" I jolted from my daydream. Lo and Harper were looking at me; their faces pinched with concern.

"Yeah. I'm good."

"You don't have to lie to us, remember? We're your girls."

"And fuck Trey, okay. I know what you're thinking about," Lo stated. "I saw the picture of them this morning in People Magazine."

"What did I miss?" Harper asked, chomping on an egg roll.

"Trey and Alyssa got married last night. And Marley, I hope you aren't blaming yourself for this."

"One thing I learned at the retreat is that people that do what Trey did to me are battling with themselves. I know it had nothing to do with me and everything to do with his own selfish reasons."

"That retreat must have taught you self-control, cause ain't no way. Ain't no fuckin' way," Harper sang in her best Future voice. "I would have crashed that wedding and whooped his ass.

We laughed.

"My little hopeless romantic," Lo squealed and caressed my cheek in such a dramatic way it made me laugh again.

"I am not."

"You are too!" Lo and Harper protested with a loud cackle.

"Marley, you've been that way for as long as I can remember."

"No matter how many times you get burned in a relationship, you never get bitter and you never stop chasing that fire."

"I agree. It's like you have this optimistic view on love," Harper added.

I was stumped by how well my friends were reading me. I recalled how the auburn loc'd therapist at the retreat told me I ignored and overlooked behavior that didn't fit my outlook on how I viewed my love interests. I dismissed their true intentions, my mind concocting my own lucid love story. I seemed to think with my heart instead of my head. With Trey, I'd thought with my heart.

"I can honestly say that the mistake I made with Trey... won't happen again. I definitely got the closure I needed," I said, thinking about my encounter with Alyssa and the vulnerable look in her eyes when she'd recognized who I was. The fact that she knew let me know that I had been a topic of conversation between her and Trey. It also felt like a high five to my ego. I was important enough to be talked about.

Harper brought up Gia again which of course brought up Jinni. Jinni was prepared to do her story in the morning with Lo and she was already acting like a diva, demanding the cover and a top-notch make-up and fashion team for her photoshoot. She was already co-writing a tell-all book with a best-selling author. Jinni was on a warpath. A woman scorned, ready to step out of the shadows as a silent housewife and show the world just how powerful she could be.

Once night had fallen, Lo and Harper left, leaving me words of advice and a coffee table littered with their crumbs and champagne flutes. I picked up their empty glasses and placed them in the dishwasher. I was throwing away the half-empty containers when there was a knock at the door. I noticed Harper's jacket and scooped it up as I headed towards the front door.

"Coming back for this?" I started, holding out her jacket, but I couldn't get the words all the way out. Standing in front of me was Trey, dressed casually in navy blue pants and a button-down.

"I was hoping the next time I saw you, you'd be in a wheelchair," I told him with a straight face.

"You sound disappointed," he chuckled nervously.

I gave him the meanest glare I could muster before I tried to shove the door closed in his face, but Trey blocked it with his hand, his strength keeping it ajar.

"Trey. Leave."

"I want to talk to you."

"Everything is about what *you* want. *I* want you to leave!"

"Marley, I'm sorry," he admitted. His blue eyes looked sincere and forlorn. I paused, focusing on him, searching his eyes, wondering why. "I hate that I hurt you. I mean that. I'm so so sorry."

"Why?" I asked, my voice just as cracked and broken as I felt inside.

Trey's eyes darted away from me. He sighed as if he was preparing for a eulogy and it reminded me of the day he broke up with me. "I can't lie to you, Marley. I never really broke up with Alyssa. I wanted to, but I never got the chance."

Hearing him say her name made me cringe.

"I didn't know how to tell her. She could sense I was having cold feet. It became a problem and it was hard for her to deal with."

"I don't care about her and how she felt. I want to know why you did this to me."

"I guess I was confused. Everything was happening so fast. Marriage... it's such a life-changing moment. It's a big step, you know," his voice cracked. "I kept struggling with whether I was making the wrong choice."

"You made me believe that I was your choice. You sounded so sure. So confident," I said, tears burning my eyelids. Trey shook his head in remorse. "I know. I know," he muttered. Silence covered us like a blanket of snow on the pavement. We held each other's gaze for a moment, questions pounding in my head. One hitting harder than the others.

"Were you dating her while you were with me, Trey?"

His eyes stretched to the top of his head. "No! I promise you."

"But you met her while you were with me, right?"

"Yeah. I did. But nothing happened between us. I never cheated on you, Marley. Alyssa and I never met up. I never called her."

"Just fell in love at first sight?" I asked confidently. "Your mother told me you were mesmerized when you saw her."

Trey looked baffled or maybe he was offended that his mother snitched on him.

"It's fine. I get it," I told him.

"No, you don't get it. Because I was in love with you and the break-up had nothing to do with you."

"Oh, I know that," I chuckled. "I was the same woman you fell in love with when you broke up with me. But I get it. You were confused then too, right. In love with two women at the same time?" I mocked.

"To put it honestly, yes."

The bit of truth ripped at me.

"You're an amazing woman, Marley." Trey sighed in his hands. "This is killing me. I feel like I made the biggest mistake ever. Losing you was..."

I held up my hand to stop the lies spewing from his mouth.

"Let me make things easier for you, Trey. I'm not confused about us at all. I don't want anything to do with you. So go home and tell your problems to your wife."

His shoulders slumped, but Trey stepped back and I was finally able to close the door.

FLIGHTS

14

Friday, January 3

My feet sprinted down the concourse like they were on a race track, dodging and weaving through the throng of people. The faster I ran, the harder my heart pounded against my chest.

"This is the final call for flight DA386. Please proceed to gate 15. The captain will be closing the doors of the aircraft in less than five minutes. I repeat, this is the final call for flight DA386."

I pushed my legs harder and faster, making my way towards gate 15.

"I'm here," I hollered, waving my hands in the air to get the attendant's attention. She looked up from her pew, but didn't look the least bit shocked. The smile on her face was sincere when I approached. I'm sure she's seen hundreds of people rushing like lunatics to catch their flight.

Gasping for air, I let out a winded *"thank goodness"* as the she scanned my boarding pass.

"Welcome aboard. Enjoy your flight," she cooed.

I nodded and re-adjusted the carry-on bag on my shoulder. I scanned the faces of passengers as I half walked, half scooted, down the long aisle. The con of booking a last-minute flight was the risk of missing out on a first-class seat. Once I found my window seat, I stuffed my duffle bag in the overhead.

The captain introduced himself and let us know that the flight would be two hours and 25 minutes. As he continued talking, I let my body melt into the more or less comfortable chair. I inhaled air through my nose and then blew it out between my lips slowly before letting my mind relax and contemplate what awaited me in a couple of hours.

I longed for the sandy beaches, fruity cocktails, a good book, and long naps. The hours of work I was putting in were mentally and physically draining me and to keep my sanity intact; a trip was much needed.

Just last week, Trey tried to make a come-back by calling my office and sending "I miss you" flowers.

The audacity!

I was so repulsed I almost threw up. I gave the flowers to a homeless woman and had my assistant Andy block his calls. I started wondering if Alyssa knew about him trying to creep back into my life. But then I realized it wasn't any of my damn business.

I was proud of myself for finally walking away from a decision that didn't suit my life. It definitely didn't bring me any peace. It made me feel weak and pathetic, but then I remembered who the fuck I was. Trey chose to do something stupid and his choice had nothing to do with me. It definitely didn't define me. I was and still am a phenomenal woman.

Phenomenal woman am I.

I shook my head and chuckled at my cheesy attempt to quote Maya Angelou.

"Wow. What are the odds?"

I looked up, surprised to see Othello putting his carry-on bag into the overhead bin. He was beaming, and I couldn't help but laugh a shocked but amused laugh. "Othello?"

I'd given up waiting for him to find me on the dating app. Hell, I'd given up on the stupid app altogether and deleted it, but that didn't stop me from thinking about him. Othello continued to cross my mind every now and again.

Othello removed his leather jacket and I wiped the drool from the side of my mouth. He looked a lot different than when I'd seen him last, at Gia's party. Gone was the distinguished gentleman look, replaced with slim-fitting jeans, suede boots, and a loose-fitted V-neck t-shirt. His muscular arms were decorated in tattoos. If I were standing, my knees would have buckled.

"What are you doing here?"

"Catching a flight to Mexico, I hope."

I laughed again at his sarcasm. He fell into the seat

next to me, his alluring cologne taking over our row and stirring something up inside of me that made me want to jump his bones.

"Marley Jacobs," he said my name as if he were impressed with it. "I thought the free coffee I got this morning would be the highlight of my day, but it's not."

"This is weird," I flushed.

"I know. But I will say, I'm glad it's you I'm sitting next to and not some old lady who snores."

I laughed again. "Stop," I pleaded.

"I'm serious. The last time I was on a plane, one fell asleep on my shoulder. Snoring, drooling, and everything," he joked. "She sounded like a freight train." Othello started making a weird groggy noise with his throat. People turned to stare and I could barely breathe from laughing so hard.

"This is wild," he said. "When you ran away from me, I honestly thought I'd never see you again."

Loud giggles kept pouring out of me and I realized it was the most I'd laughed in months. "I didn't run away," I cackled. "I *walked* away to take a phone call."

"Yeah, but you never came back," he stated. Othello's eyes scanned my breast and my nipples got hard. I thought he was being perverted, but I realized he wasn't being fresh at all. He was just scanning the writing on my shirt. "Catch flights, not feelings?" he read.

I perked up a shoulder until it grazed my cheek and smiled. "Yep."

"Damn. So, I guess I don't stand a chance, huh?"

"You don't stand a chance," I kidded. I said it with a smile. Othello smiled too.

"Maybe I'll just try my luck anyway," he murmured. The way he looked at me was so piercing I had to look away. I listened to him put on his seat belt while I squeezed my knees together.

By then, the flight attendant was going over all safety protocols and pointing out all the exits on the plane.

"What's waiting for you in Mexico? Or should I say *who*?" Othello asked.

My neck stretched back and I gave Othello a salty look. "The beach is waiting for me in Mexico. Frozen alcoholic drinks with umbrellas in them. Peace of mind. No distractions. That's what's waiting for me in Mexico."

"Here you go," he chuckled.

"I'm just saying. A woman can't just go on vacation alone? They need a man to travel?"

Othello cracked up, holding his side. "You're killing me! I didn't say anything like that."

"Maybe not, but don't lie, you were thinking it."

"Okay, yeah. I was for a second, but I'm glad to see that you're not."

"I'm definitely not," I said in a snooty voice. "If anything, I should be asking who you are meeting in Mexico. I saw your profile on Hooked."

"Hooked?" he questioned and looked off with furrowed brows. "Oh, that dating app? I haven't been on there in months. I meant to delete that shit."

I gave him a major side-eye. He chuckled again,

always chuckling. Not only was it infectious, but it was also cute. "I kid you not. I don't use that app."

"Really?"

"Really. And my cousin is getting married at the Azulik resort. I hear it's phenomenal... what?" he asked when he saw me cover my face with shame.

"I too, am staying at the Azulik resort."

"You're kidding me?"

"I kid you not," I said, stealing his own words. He took notice and smirked.

I stole a glance out the window and shrieked at the realization that the plane was at the runway waiting for its turn to take off. I'd been so engrossed in conversation with Othello that I forgot to start my breathing exercises and pray. Anxiety danced inside my body and I gripped the armrest on my seat.

"I'd love to take you to dinner or drinks sometime during your stay."

I had been trying to brace myself for take-off, but his suggestion broke my bearing.

"You have to eat on this peaceful, self-care, all about you, vacation, right?" He asked, staring at me. "How long are you staying?"

"What part of no distractions didn't you understand?" I quipped.

Othello pressed his large manly fingers into his chest. "I'm a distraction?"

I nodded.

In more ways than one.

I wiggled around in my chair to get comfortable and soothe my tension.

"The only way I would be a distraction for you is if you felt some type of way about me."

His words caught me off guard and I looked him in the eye, trying my hardest to be disgusted, but it wasn't working. I cracked a smile.

The plane revved up and I tried to get back to forgetting I was on a plane. I closed my eyes and took a deep breath as I imagined myself in a safe, comfy place.

"You okay?" Othello asked.

I ignored him, but not to be rude. I had to stay centered. I kept my head pressed back into the seat, my eyes clenched tight. I could hear the engine growling louder and louder, ready to pick up momentum. The worst part of the plane ride for me was the takeoff; it always made my nerves twitchy. I braced myself for the lift, wishing I had remembered to take that sleeping pill when I'd parked my car at the airport. Rushing made me forget all about it. I usually dozed off right before the plane took off.

When I felt Othello's hand brush the top of mine, it sent a shock wave through me so sharp that I snapped my eyes open. I turned to him. His eyes gazed back into mine. Nothing needed to be said as we stared at each other, a mixture of desire and understanding.

"I got you," he said to me, a warm smile plastered on his sexy ass face. When he realized I wasn't going to pull away from him, Othello intertwined our fingers together, and just like that, my anxiety seemed to calm down. He gave it a gentle squeeze and I closed my eyes.

The plane pushed us back gently as it jetted off down the runway. I could feel us leaving the ground, floating up, up, and away.

"So..." Othello questioned.

I opened one eye and peeked at him. "So?"

"Dinner? With me? In Mexico?"

I didn't think twice. "Yes. I'd love that."

Othello grinned triumphantly and caressed my hand with his thumb.

I pressed my eyes shut again, a smile slowly spreading across my face. The tension in my body evaporated, settling into relaxation mode as we floated on, gliding smoothly through the clouds, en route to paradise.

ACKNOWLEDGMENTS

Wow. I finally published my first book guys!!! I couldn't sleep last night thinking about this moment.

Special thanks to my editors, Brandi and Hoffman. Brandi, you were so encouraging, and I appreciate you being with The Marley Diaries from the beginning.

Thank you, thank you, Murphy Rae, for this beautiful cover. I wasn't sure which way to go with this book, but your creative mind concocted this a masterpiece.

Huge thanks to Taaffe Theriot and Taquelah Blue for naming Othello Kingston. He is so delicious!

I am also thankful for all the beautiful supporters that were there for Marley when she was just a chapter a week on Facebook: Erica Scriven, Stasia Jordan, Rachel Williams, Karshundra Mack, Chaquita Willis, Talajah McCloud, Andrea Williams, Shakeema Warren, Donika Ashley, Serenity Centeria, Kia Thomas, Dewaun Jennings, Tae Davis, Lachell Murphy, Tony Wayne Spearman, Jackie Brown, and Bert Wil. Thank you guys for motivating me while I worked on this story week after week. (I sure do miss Marley Mondays)

Christy Taylor Baskin for loving this story so much that you decided to interview me and have me on your show!! You had me feeling like a superstar!

Huge thanks to my dear friend, Joy Knight Harris. You marketed this book better than I did. You even mapped out what to do and say up until release day. I love you so much!

To my mom and my sister for playing my beta readers, editors, and therapist. Y'all are the real MVPs. Thank you for always ALWAYS being there for me. I don't know what I would do without you two in my life.

To my beautiful creations, Javin, Nichelle, Gabrielle, and Nicholas. Y'all are my best friends. Having you is my greatest achievement.

To everyone that supported me through my writing journey, I thank you so much for not giving up on me! I can't name you all, and if I forgot anyone please blame my mind and not my heart.

Finally, to my father, brother, and grandmother who passed away, I am still broken without you guys. I miss you all so much. Wish you were here for this, but I know you see me.

ABOUT THE AUTHOR

Vasalona Cooper has been a great teller of stories since the first grade. She has gone on to write for local magazines and has had her work published in Cosmopolitan. Aside from writing, Vasalona loves to play in beauty products, travel, bake, and hang out with her children in Savannah, GA.

You can follow her on Instagram

@vasalonacooper

Made in the USA
Columbia, SC
21 February 2022